OTHER
Harlequin Romances
by ELIZABETH ASHTON

Many of these titles are available at your local bookseller
or through the Harlequin Reader Service.

For a free catalogue listing all available Harlequin Romances,
send your name and address to:

HARLEQUIN READER SERVICE,
M.P.O. Box 707, Niagara Falls, N.Y. 14302
Canadian address: Stratford, Ontario, Canada N5A 6W2

or use order coupon at back of book.

Breeze from the Bosphorous

by

ELIZABETH ASHTON

Harlequin Books

TORONTO • LONDON • NEW YORK • AMSTERDAM • SYDNEY

Original hardcover edition published in 1977
by Mills & Boon Limited

ISBN 0-373-02172-0

Harlequin edition published June 1978

PRINTED IN U.S.A.

CHAPTER ONE

THE close friendship between Venice Franklin and Selma Hadleigh that lasted for so many years was always a puzzle to their mutual acquaintances and could be only accounted for as the attraction of opposites. They came from different backgrounds, their circumstances were totally dissimilar, and they were completely unalike in appearance and temperament. They had met at school.

In after years Selma often described her first impression of Venice with a slight touch of malice, that Venice did not resent. She herself was always astonished that Selma had been drawn to her.

'She was a pale wisp of a creature,' Selma would remember. 'A pathetic little waif, with her hair scraped back and her uniform too big for her, who looked as if she expected everyone to bite her. Of course I felt I had to take her under my wing, it was the humane thing to do.'

Selma was beautiful, effervescent, good-natured and irresponsible, but she remained loyal to Venice throughout their schooldays and beyond. Venice, who actually was a year older than Selma, possessed the stronger character, and once the initial strangeness wore off began to emerge as a personality. She was good at her lessons and helped Selma with her homework, for though her friend had flashes of brilliance, she lacked concentration. Venice pushed her through her examinations and Selma swore eternal gratitude, but when the elder girls attempted to tease Venice, Selma flew to her defence with a fury that intimidated them, and Venice was in her turn duly thankful.

Selma's favourite game was to plan the wonderful things they would do when they had left boarding school. Venice played up to her, though, more realistic than her friend, she feared their paths were likely to diverge when they went out into the world.

'I'll have to work for my living,' she told Selma, for that had been pointed out to her when she started school with the injunction to work hard, for the fees for the somewhat expensive boarding school were being paid for by her dead father's insurance money and there would be nothing left by the time she completed her education.

'And you'll be living in the lap of luxury,' she concluded; a cliché that was appropriate, for the Hadleighs were rich.

'But we'll still be friends,' Selma insisted, 'and I'll give you everything you want.'

Selma was as generous as she was beautiful.

'You've given me what's worth more than all the money in the world,' Venice assured her. 'Friendship and love.'

For those two invaluable gifts had been sadly lacking in her young life. She had been brought up by her aunt since she was an infant of five years old. Her parents had perished in a sailing accident, a source of grievance to Joan Franklin, who regarded such recreation as extravagant and foolish and characteristic of her sister-in-law, Rosemary, who she considered to be a feckless creature and quite unworthy of her adored younger brother. When the tragedy occurred she found herself guardian of a child she neither wanted nor could love, but it was a responsibility she would not dream of shirking, for she had a stern sense of duty. It was astonishing that this sour puritanical woman could be Derek Franklin's sister, for he had been a gay and extrovert young man, but she was years older than he, and having no other kin, their parents had died young, she adored her young brother with a fierce and possessive passion. His marriage was a bitter blow to her and she was determined to eradicate or at least to subdue the natural gaiety and high spirits her niece had inherited from her parents. Even her name was an offence.

'Ridiculous!' Joan Franklin had snorted. 'To call a girl after a town, and a decadent sort of place too from what I've heard. You must change it to Vera, which is what I shall call you.'

But Venice clung to her name. She knew Rosemary had given it to her because she had spent her honeymoon in that city and had fallen in love with its drowned beauty, though she was glad she had been spared the Italian version. Venezia would have been too much of a good thing. She could be obstinate where her feelings were concerned and after some confusion over school entries etc, for Venice was the name on her birth certificate, her aunt gave in, but she herself never called her anything except Vera.

Selma had applauded her tenacity. 'The name suits you somehow,' she had declared. 'It has a sort of wistful watery sound and it's original. You wouldn't be you if you were called Sarah or Deborah.'

'My looks hardly merit it,' Venice had complained despondently, for she was a quiet apathetic child whose eyes looked out on the world with puzzled bewilderment, wondering why she had had to lose her lovely, laughing mother, whose memory became fainter every year, however desperately she clung to it, to be put in the charge of her grim, stern aunt. Joan never praised her or gave her any sign of affection, but fed and clothed her in plain unbecoming garments as a painful duty. She packed her off to boarding school as soon as she was old enough, saying she would be glad to get her from under her feet.

'Oh, I don't know.' Selma, who had been born with dress sense, studied her friend consideringly. 'Well groomed and in pretty clothes you could look very attractive. You'll have to break through those repressions your aunt has engendered that make you scuttle about like a frightened mouse. You don't know how animation becomes you. As soon as you're free of her, I'll take you in hand and you won't know yourself.'

Selma too was motherless, which was an additional bond between them. Yasmin Hadleigh had died at her birth, she had been a frail beauty from the Middle East whom her father had met during his travels. Lucas Hadleigh was a brilliant and versatile man. He had attained the highest academic honours, had studied chemistry and science, been director of several colleges, but resigned in favour of lecturing when he inherited a quite substantial fortune mostly lodged in Swiss banks. His hobbies included archaeology and ancient history. He maintained a flat in London where Selma spent her holidays in the care of an indulgent housekeeper, since he was usually away, and there Venice joined her whenever possible. Fortunately her aunt did not veto these visits, for she liked to impress her cronies by boasting about her niece's connection with the wealthy and well known Hadleighs, but she was always warning Venice that her circumstances were different from Selma's and she must not get ideas above her station.

Venice found in the Hadleigh household the warmth and colour so lacking in her own, and thought it was the right setting for her friend. Selma was a dark beauty with blue-black hair inherited from her Eastern mother. She had an oval face and a flawless skin, big lustrous eyes and a mouth like a flower. Her figure even

8

in her early teens was delicately rounded, while Venice stayed flat as a boy. She possessed that indefinable quality known as sex-appeal and boys gravitated towards her like wasps to jam. Venice was the recipient of many confidences about Selma's adolescent fancies, but they were no more than that. She would be wildly enamoured of some quite unsuitable youth for perhaps a week, then she would find faults in him and finally say:

'I don't think I like him after all.'

Venice, much more level-headed, managed to extricate her from the many scrapes her rash impetuosity landed her into. Professor Hadleigh more than once asked her to keep an eye upon his wayward daughter.

'You seem to be the only person who has any influence over her,' he told her. 'I rely upon you to restrain her.'

A small price to pay for the lavish hospitality of his flat, but ...

'Your father seems to think I'm a prig,' she complained.

Selma laughed, her rich sexy laugh. 'You're not a prig, darling. What he means is you've got your head screwed on tight, while mine always wobbles. You're my good angel, Ven.'

Venice decided she would train to be a teacher, and her aunt approved of her choice. To her surprise Selma elected to train also in the hope that they would obtain places in the same college.

'Pa says I must do something to use my brain,' she explained. 'But I'm not as clever as he is. You'll have to get me through the exams somehow, Ven.'

They both graduated and obtained places at the same college, much to their delight.

During their last school holidays, prior to becoming students, Professor Hadleigh took his daughter on a

9

tour of Anatolia to see the ruins of Troy. He asked Venice to accompany them, but her aunt would not hear of it.

'Nasty insanitary places,' she had declared. 'You're not going out there to catch some disgusting disease!'

So Venice had to spend the holiday at home doing household chores for her aunt with only Selma's picture postcards to console her. It was doubly hard upon her because she was eager to travel, and Troy was to her a magic word. Selma upon her return was scornful about it.

'Just a heap of dreary old stones,' she described it.

She was too excited about their new life and the students' hostel where they were to stay to say much about her holiday, but she did mention a family called Osman who had a house beside the Bosphorus.

'Some sort of cousins of my mother,' she explained vaguely. 'There were two sons, one about my age, the other a bit older—Ahmet and Kemal. I wasn't allowed to be alone with them, so I couldn't get to know them.' She giggled. 'Ahmet was quite handsome,' she added pensively.

Venice had no premonition that the names would ever mean anything more to her than just that— names.

The beautiful Selma naturally made a great impact upon the male students and even the staff, but she seemed indifferent to the admiration she aroused. She flirted innocently with a few of the more presentable young men, but she was critical of them. Either they bored her with their enthusiasms or repelled her by too blatant advances.

'Most of them are too hairy,' she told Venice with a shiver. 'I hate hirsute men, and I like fellows to be well groomed.'

Oddly enough it was Venice who formed an attachment and not the lovely Selma. William Perrin, or Bill as he was usually called, was also a student, a good-looking rather serious young man, whose subject was mathematics. He was something of a sportsman, being devoted to climbing, fishing and tennis. Venice played the game too, and that was how their friendship started. Selma did not care for games and was not impressed by Bill. Neither did he admire Selma.

'Too foreign-looking,' was his comment.

'Too English and earnest,' was her description of him.

But they often formed a foursome with Selma's current escort and had a great deal of fun together.

College for Venice had meant freedom from Joan Franklin's surveillance, but her aunt gave her a piti-fully small allowance. She would have had a thin time of it but for Selma's generosity. Selma was adept at finding ways and means of paying her expenses without offending her pride. Once she said:

'Except for Pa you're the only person I care about and I can't be happy while you're skimped, and you're much more deserving than I am.'

The holidays Venice spent in the Hadleighs' flat. Sometimes the Professor was there, more often not. He was becoming more and more interested in his archaeo-logical research and tried to persuade his daughter to accompany him upon a dig, but she refused.

'Pa dear, I need my holidays to relax. Somehow I've got to finish up with a diploma if only to satisfy Ven, and the effort will absorb all my energies.'

The last term was a strenuous time for both of them, for Venice was determined to obtain honours and Selma did not want to disgrace herself.

At length it was all over, their qualifications in the can, by which time the Professor had retired and bought a house on the Bosphorus where he proposed to live permanently. Venice was dismayed. If he gave up the London flat she would lose what she had always looked upon as her real home.

'Don't worry, he'll probably change his mind,' Selma said comfortably. Unfortunately he did not.

It was the first day of the holidays upon which the blow fell. Venice was leaving shortly for a week's camping with Bill and Selma was waiting to hear her father's plans. As it was the housekeeper's afternoon off, Venice was making a cup of tea, while Selma sprawled on the divan in the sitting room. The afternoon post arrived with an airmail letter for Selma and Venice carried it in with the tray of tea.

'From Pa,' Selma said languidly, slitting it open. 'Excuse me.'

Venice poured out the tea, thinking how decorative her friend looked amid the oriental draperies spread over the big divan. The whole room was exotic with the many trophies the Professor had brought back from his wanderings. Grecian urns stood in corners, onyx and jade ornaments filled Chinese cabinets; the carpet was Turkish, the curtains heavy velvet. There was no attempt at orderly arrangement, but the whole effect was rich and comfortable. She had always loved Selma's home and she wondered if she could ask her friend to allow her to stay at the flat when she had returned from her week's camping with Bill, until she herself returned to join her. She would need a base while she applied for work, and she did not want to stay with her aunt.

Selma dropped the letter and looked ruefully at Venice.

'Pa has for once made up his mind,' she told her. 'He's instructed an agent to sub-let this flat. I knew Mrs Proctor'—the housekeeper—'has been muttering about going to live with a sister who has a small business, but didn't know her departure was imminent. Apparently she's told Pa she's going. He's decided we're to live permanently in Rumelia, that's the European part of Turkey.'

'Oh dear!' Venice passed her the cup of tea that she had poured out, aware of a sinking heart. She had expected that Selma would be returning after the holidays, and they had even hoped they might be appointed to the same school.

'Bit of a knock-out, isn't it?' Selma said, looking round the room. 'I'm fond of this place.'

'So am I,' Venice sighed, unable to visualise life without the Hadleighs and the sanctuary of their home. 'But your training, Sel, aren't you going to do anything with it?'

'Not if I can help it,' Selma replied, stirring her tea. She looked lovely and exotic in a red kaftan she often wore in the house, with her rich hair loose upon her shoulders, and not in the least like the conventional idea of a schoolteacher. 'Oh, Pa's got some bee in his bonnet about teaching English in Turkey—the people next door, the Osmans, they're connected with my mother's people, I believe I told you, are keen on modernising Turkey and all that lark. He thinks that now I've qualified I could help if I want something to do out there.' She curled her lip disdainfully. 'He's got another think coming. I only trained because I wanted to be with you.'

'Very sweet of you, but not a good reason for dedicating yourself to teaching.'

'Dedicated nothing! I had to do something. Pa says every woman should have a profession to fall back upon, but I'd prefer to fall back upon a wealthy husband if the need ever arose.'

Venice was certain Selma would marry, but the more immediate subject was her departure for Turkey and if she were going to live there permanently, they would be parted. Without her companionship, her life would be bleak. Selma's thoughts were on another track.

'I've just realised Pa hopes that I will eventually marry one of the Osmans. He's quite crazy about Turkey and talks of becoming naturalised. Once arranged marriages were the rule out there, but not nowadays, thank goodness. I'd hate to have my husband chosen for me.'

'Who wouldn't!' Venice exclaimed.

Selma was looking pensive. 'If they've turned out presentable, I might consider marrying one of them. It would be better than teaching. Both apparently are candidates for my lily-white hand. But I only had a glimpse of them when I was out there. Pa was very thick with old Osman and I was taken to see him. He died recently and there's a widowed mother, who thinks all young girls should still be kept in purdah, or that was the impression she gave me. She'd be rather a drawback, but it might be fun playing Ahmet off against Kemal and vice versa—those are their names, did I tell you?'

But Venice ignored this typically Selma remark to exclaim incredulously;

'But you'd never consider marrying a Turk?'

Selma laughed. 'You're forgetting I'm half one myself. They're quite Westernised nowadays, darling, no harems and only one wife. A lot work abroad, and bring back foreign wives whom their families have to accept.' She put down her cup and looked at Venice mischievously. 'You marry Kemal, and I'll marry Ahmet, how's that for an idea?'

'A quite absurd one. A, I'm not going out to Turkey and B, there's Bill.'

'I'm sure a young Turk would be much more amusing than Bill, and of course you're coming with me.

You've all the summer holidays before you, and you can surely spare me a few weeks?'

'It's sweet of you to think of it, but I can't—it's much too expensive for one thing.'

'Of course you'd come as my guest.'

'Thank you, darling, but I can't always be sponging on you.' Venice stood up and moved restlessly about the room looking sadly at each familiar object. 'I suppose the break had to come some time, but oh, Sel, I'll miss you so!'

'Dear Ven, always so intense,' Selma murmured. 'But we're not parted yet.' She referred to her letter. 'Pa asks you to come out with me, he says you'll be very welcome. Wouldn't you like to see Istanbul?'

'I'd love to, but I'm going camping with Bill.'

'You can do that any time, surely he'll understand this is a chance not to be missed? You must come, Ven, I'll need you to support me among all these strangers. Pa's so vague he'll involve me with these weird characters against my will before I know where I am. You see, I'm not supposed to mention this, but I believe he's engaged in some financial deal with the Osmans, and they may consider me part of the bargain. I may find I don't like the set-up at all and I want someone on my side. Don't let me down, Ven.'

Her big dark eyes were wide and coaxing. When Selma wanted her own way, she went on wheedling until she got it.

'Apparently they're your own kin,' Venice returned drily. 'You'll hardly need protecting from them, and you'll have to make your home out there if this place is to be let.'

'If I don't like it, I'll come back and we'll have a home together,' Selma announced, ignoring the impracticability of this idea. She sat up with sudden energy. 'I've always been a good friend to you, haven't I?'

15

'The very best,' Venice agreed fervently.

'Then don't refuse me now. I really need you, I can't face the journey out there alone. I'm sure to lose my passport, mislay my ticket or get abducted. It's not safe for me to go by myself, and Pa thinks so too.'

Venice knew there was a possibility of all three catastrophes occurring. Selma could be very careless and was far too trusting with strangers. She was strongly tempted, for she had always longed to travel and Istanbul had a magical sound.

'I don't like letting Bill down,' she objected.

'Oh, he'll understand,' Selma said easily, 'or if he doesn't he'll be very selfish. You wouldn't want to tie yourself to a selfish man, darling?'

Venice laughed. 'I'm not tied to him at all ... yet.'

'Well then?' Venice hesitated, finding it difficult to resist the appeal in her friend's eyes. 'Pa's made the reservations through an agency and the tickets are being sent to me,' Selma went on. 'It would be such a waste if yours isn't used.'

Venice was touched by this generosity which would relieve her of any expense, though she thought the Professor had been rash to take her consent for granted.

'In that case I'll come,' she said, 'providing I can square Bill. That is if you're sure you really want me?'

'Of course I want you, and I'll want your opinion of my cousins and which one will make the best husband.'

'Then you *are* seriously considering his wishes?'

'Naturally—I'm a dutiful daughter.' Selma's eyes twinkled wickedly. 'The Osmans are very well off, and I wouldn't mind living in the lap of luxury with a handsome male to look after me.'

Venice smiled; she was used to Selma's fluctuating moods. Privately she thought her friend was born to be some man's cherished wife, and teaching was not her métier at all. But she had been brought up in England as an English girl, and to take on a foreigner was a hazardous proceeding.

'I hope you won't commit yourself in a hurry,' she said warningly. 'It's a big step to marry a man of another nationality and accept his country instead of your own.'

'Oh, I know quite a lot about Turkey,' Selma told her with a charming air of superiority. 'To begin with, since you'll meet the Osmans—they live next door— Turks use the first name with the addition of *bey* for men and *hanim* for women. You'll address Mrs Osman as Zubeyde Hanim.'

'Oh, will I?' Venice was a little taken aback.

'You see, prior to the revolution a lot of Turks didn't have surnames,' Selma went on, pleased to be able to impart information to her more erudite friend. 'But Mustapha Kemal made family names obligatory and took that of Ataturk for himself. It means Father of the Turks.'

'Really?' Venice did not know much about the Turkish revolution.

'What we call the Golden Horn, they call the Halic, the Bosphorus is the Bogazici. Turkey is Turkiye, the Black Sea the Kara Deniz ...'

'Stop showing off,' Venice interrupted. 'I don't suppose I'm expected to learn the language. I believe it's difficult.'

'It is,' Selma agreed, 'that's why I haven't picked it up, but I suppose I'll have to if I marry Ahmet—or Kemal. But nearly everyone speaks English in Rumelia, that's Turkey in Europe. Of course in the wilds of Anatolia they're not so educated, but we shan't be going there.'

'What a pity!' Venice was beginning to feel excited and adventurous now she had decided to accept Selma's offer. She would like to explore the whole of this strange land to which she hoped to go. She would ring Bill to meet her in their usual coffee bar and she hoped he would be sympathetic to her change of plan. He must realise a few weeks in Istanbul was not a bonus that was likely to come her way again.

'Istanbul, whew!' Bill Perrin gave a whistle. 'Minarets and mosques, the Golden Horn, shades of sultanas and the seraglio. Also, I expect sunshine. Very different from this.' He glanced at the café windows down which, although it was summer, cold rain was pouring down the panes. 'I can see why you want to go, Ven, but is it wise?'

Venice took a sip of her coffee and glanced thoughtfully at the young man sitting opposite to her. Selma could not accuse Bill of being hirsute, he was clean-shaven with that fresh boyish look common to so many British youths. Some day they expected to drift into marriage when they had sufficient savings. She knew his question about wisdom was prompted by the fact that they both had to find employment amidst the diminishing demand for teachers now that they had finished their courses. Without this invitation a holiday in Turkey would be impossible for years to come. She had expected Bill to make objections, and fond as she was of him she was a little irritated by his cautiousness.

'It'll only be for a few weeks,' she pointed out. 'And I would like to oblige Selma Hadleigh. As you know, the Hadleighs have been awfully good to me. The Professor wants me to look after her on the journey.'

'Can't she look after herself?'

'No. You know Selma.'

'I do—quite irresponsible. Don't you go letting her lead you into mischief.'

'It'll be my job to keep her out of it.'

18

'I believe you think more of Selma than you do of me,' Bill grumbled.

'Don't be absurd!' Venice laughed. 'But you must admit I've known her considerably longer. Anyway, if Professor Hadleigh really means to make his home at this place on the Bosphorus, I shan't be seeing much more of Selma.'

A shadow crossed her mobile face, because she would sorely miss her friend.

'You'll have me to console you,' Bill reassured her.

'I'm thankful for that.' Venice stretched out her hand across the table between them, and after a moment's hesitation, he took it in his. Bill was oddly conventional for this day and age and disliked demonstrations in public. Not that he was ever very lavish with them in private, Venice thought ruefully, though she admired his restraint. Since they could not marry for some years, it was better to be circumspect.

'I'm sorry about our week's camping,' she told him, for they had planned to spend the first week of their holiday in Wales. 'But we can go another year and as a lot of your sporting pals will be there, you won't miss me.'

She was not very keen on such diversions herself, disliking the confines of a tent, but they were inexpensive, and Bill, a keen sportsman, was looking forward to climbing the Welsh mountains.

'It won't be the same without you,' Bill declared with transparent insincerity. 'Of course it can't compare with the glamour of Istanbul. All right, Ven, if you want to go, I won't stand in your way, though I never understand the fascination of foreign places myself. I'd much rather stay in Britain.'

'Not very enterprising, are you, Bill?'

'Well, there are lots of pretty places in the British Isles to see first without all the trouble of passports, air

19

travel, strange languages and food to cope with.'

'But, Bill darling, all that is fun and it makes such a change.'

'It just doesn't appeal to me, so you'd better get rid of your wanderlust before we're married, then you'll be ready to settle down.'

'And reconcile myself to Brighton and Eastbourne?' She laughed, then sobered. 'You talk about being married, but we aren't even engaged.'

'Time enough for that,' Bill remarked. 'Once I put a ring on your finger everyone'll start enquiring about the wedding. I've got to get established before I can take a wife, and even with us both working it'll take time to save for a deposit on a house and all the other things.'

'Always so practical!' she sighed.

'We have to be sensible.'

He was quite right, but sometimes she wished he would be less sensible and more romantic, but with her ingrained lack of confidence, thanks to her aunt's criticisms, she was flattered to have acquired a boyfriend who wanted to marry her. Selma was a little contemptuous about Bill, declaring he was not exciting. Venice had returned that he was more likely to make a good husband if he was not. She found his company comfortable and congenial and they were both interested in the problems of modern education. Also, having been deprived of affection in her childhood, she responded to it like an opening flower. Bill was very fond of her, but he was scornful about romantic love.

'We're two modern well adjusted young people,' he was fond of stating. 'We can dispense with the sentimental rot youngsters call love. They inflame themselves with a lot of erotic twaddle that only leads them into difficulties.'

Emotionally undeveloped, Venice had agreed, relieved that Bill made so few demands upon her. Neither had any wish for pre-marital adventures. Bill declared they were cheap and rubbed the bloom off; he preferred to wait. Venice again agreed, respecting him for his high principles. But Selma had scoffed at them.

'That one has no passion,' she declared. 'Except for football matches.'

Venice had of course defended him, but now she was wishing that Bill occasionally showed a little more ardour; he expended far more enthusiasm upon his sport than upon her. She wondered if Selma was right and his feelings for her were only tepid.

'Perhaps it's as well neither of us is passionate,' she observed, watching him closely for his reaction.

'What's that remark in aid of?' he demanded belligerently.

'Well, if we were, we might find a long wait a bit trying.'

'Oh, really, Ven!' Bill exclaimed disgustedly. 'What's come over you? You know I hold no brief for the permissive age. I have, I hope, plenty of self-control and you're a nice, respectable girl. I wouldn't dream of debauching you.'

Venice laughed merrily. 'Debauch! What a lovely word. I'm not sure what it means.'

'Of course you know,' he said sharply. 'But I was drawn to you because you're so fresh and innocent. I don't like forward girls.'

'Sounds Victorian,' Venice commented moodily. It was true that she had not had much experience with boys during her adolescence, circumstances had prohibited it, and Bill had claimed her soon after she had gone to college. Promiscuity had revolted her and the few kisses that had come her way left her unmoved, but she did not quite like Bill's description of her. She was immaculate through choice not lack of opportunity.

Bill was eyeing her with faint disapproval. She had very fair hair, almost silver-gilt in some lights, a pale delicate skin and fine bones. Her best feature was her eyes, long green eyes fringed with dark lashes, which could look provocative, but she rarely permitted them to do so. She was of medium height with a slim boyish figure. Occasionally when she was animated her face would flash into transient beauty, but normally she was too pale and quiet to be noticeable. Bill appreciated her because she was a good listener and he did not want her to appear conspicuous. There had been a hint of revolt in her last remarks which had disturbed him. It was out of character. Becoming aware of his expression, she said gently:

'I didn't mean to needle you. I'm a bit excited about Istanbul, that's all.'

'Is that so?' He sounded relieved. 'Well I hope it turns out to be as glamorous as you expect. I know I can always trust you in the Orient or anywhere else.' His thin-lipped mouth curved in a smile. 'You're not likely to fall for a Turk.'

'A quite revolting idea!' Venice laughed. 'Exotic foreigners have no appeal for me. You're my man, Bill, and I'll never betray your trust.'

She believed what she said, having little self-knowledge. She was unaware of the passionate emotions lying dormant in her being, waiting to be called to birth and which Bill had failed to touch.

CHAPTER TWO

THERE was no one to meet the two girls at the airport and Selma, who had been expecting her father, was annoyed.

'I hope he hasn't forgotten we're coming,' she grumbled. 'I wouldn't put it past him.'

It had been Venice's first experience of flying and she had not altogether enjoyed it. She had been a little nervous and they had encountered several air pockets. When they landed her ears felt as if they were stuffed with cotton wool and everything seemed to be a little remote.

Bill had come to see them off, and she had again apologised for letting him down over the camping, but he had brushed her contrition aside.

'Oh, don't worry about that,' he had said cheerfully. 'There'll be other fellows at the camp and I'll be fishing and climbing, which aren't your cup of tea.'

It occurred to her that far from regretting her absence, he was relieved that she was not going with him and he could concentrate upon his favourite ploys without considering her, which though it soothed her conscience was a little dampening.

He gave her a chaste peck upon her cheek with a muttered, 'Have a good time,' when they parted in reception and hurried away—almost, she thought, with alacrity.

'Not a very ardent lover, your Bill,' Selma remarked as they waited for their flight.

Venice was thinking rather the same thing, but she hastened to defend him.

'He's known me quite a while and I'm no oil painting,' she pointed out. 'It's glamorous women like you who inspire violent passions, and I'd as soon do without them.'

Selma gave her an oblique look, but said nothing. Venice was looking very attractive in a thin cream travelling coat and a straw hat, for she had been warned she would need its shade when she arrived, and she disliked dark glasses. If she had not been eclipsed by Selma's startling beauty, she would have had her share of admiring glances, but Selma in black pants and a scarlet tabard, with a black sombrero topping her mass of hair, drew all masculine eyes in their vicinity.

Since there was no one to escort them upon arrival, Selma insisted upon taking a taxi, though Venice murmured that it would be expensive, as they were a long way out of the town and they ought to take the bus.

'Oh, hang the expense,' Selma exclaimed irritably. 'I'm not going to stew in a bus. If Pa complains it's his own fault, he should have been here. If he hasn't got a car he could have borrowed the Osmans'.'

Venice's spirits revived as her ears became unstuck, and they traversed the city with its mingling of old and new, mostly new in their case as their route took them along the modern boulevards. There were mosques everywhere with their domes and minarets piercing the skyline. Though Istanbul boasts of being built upon seven hills, age had flattened them considerably.

'Pa says the Turks are good drivers,' Selma remarked as their chauffeur threaded his way through the dense traffic towards the bridge over the Golden Horn. 'All the bad ones are dead.'

'That's something to be thankful for,' Venice responded, 'though the reason sounds a bit macabre.' She

24

rather doubted the accuracy of the Professor's statement, for many of the drivers of other vehicles seemed bent upon suicide.

The Golden Horn was thronged with shipping and a cruise liner was berthed by the Galata Bridge, together with the laden ferries that plied between the Rumelian and the Anatolian coasts, and the several islands. Over all lay a hot blue sky, reflected in the water.

The taxi turned left along the banks of the Bosphorus, where the shore was lined with cafés, hotels and fishing boats, and drove past the long wall of the huge Dolmabahce Palace. On the side furthest from the water, the land was hilly and in places rose steeply, covered with trees and shrubs.

They passed under the new suspension bridge that links Europe and Asia, built high enough to allow ships bound to and from the Black Sea to pass beneath it, a stupendous piece of engineering, carrying its double lanes of cars, past the impressive pile of the Rumeli Hisar, an ancient castle, then turning inland, their taxi came to a halt before a white villa set back from the road, and their driver hastened to open the door for them.

'You 'ave arrived, ladies. 'Ere is ze Villa Yasmin.'

The girls got out and he went to fetch their cases from the boot. They walked up the steep tiled path to the house, for the house was set on a little rise. All the green-latticed shutters were firmly closed, bees droned among the flowery shrubs in front of it, and the villa drowsed in the afternoon sun without a sign of life. The driver dumped their cases on the doorstep and pressed the bell. They could hear it ringing in what appeared to be an empty house. No one came to answer it.

'I suppose this is the right place?' Venice asked uneasily. There was something daunting about this apparently deserted residence.

'Of course it is.' Selma was tired, hot and cross. 'Villa Yasmin.' It was written beside the front door. 'It was my mother's name.'

Their driver nodded sympathetically. 'Zis is right, Ze Ciragan Caddesi, ze Professor Bey, 'e live 'ere—yes, yes, I know, 'e famous man.'

'Must have gone out and forgotten all about us,' Selma said disgustedly. She took out her purse and paid the man an immense sum in Turkish money, it seemed to Venice. She was too tired to bargain with him, though he had probably overcharged. But he lingered, loth to leave them stranded, and rang the bell again.

'It's no use,' Selma told him. 'He's not here now.'

'Selma Hanim?'

A young man had appeared round the side of the villa and was staring at Selma. The Ottoman Turks have become a very mixed race, they are all shapes and sizes, fair and dark. This one was dark, with almost classical features, suggesting Greek blood somewhere in his ancestry. He was tall, lithe and slim, wearing a white linen suit. His really magnificent black eyes were fixed admiringly on Selma.

'That's my name,' she said shortly.

He turned to the taxi driver with a snap of his fingers, dismissing him with a phrase in Turkish. 'All is well,' he added for the girls' benefit.

'All is not well,' Selma snapped. 'I want a drink and I need a bath. We can't get in.' She had tried the door and it was locked.

'That will be attended to if you will come with me.' His English was nearly perfect with only a slight accent, but spoken with the precision of one who had learned an alien tongue. 'My mother will receive you. Your father is not at home.'

'That's obvious,' she said rudely. Then as she took in the young man's good looks, she gave him a slow smile.

'Are you by any chance one of the Osmans?'

He inclined his head. 'Ahmet, your cousin.'

'Only a distant one.' She held out her hand and he hesitated, then he shook it. 'The British way, naturally.'

'Naturally.' He relinquished it reluctantly.

Venice had stood aloof throughout this conversation. Ahmet had not given her as much as a glance. She too was tired and thirsty, longing to get into the shade. Professor Hadleigh had been very remiss to have forgotten their arrival, but there was something ominous about that empty house that caused a chill. Surely if Lucas Hadleigh had gone out there would be a maid, a housekeeper, someone to receive them? He could not live in it alone.

Selma remembered her existence.

'This is my friend, Venice.'

Ahmet gave her a cursory glance, bowed slightly, but neither of them extended a hand.

'If you will come with me,' he invited, 'you shall have the drink and the bath. We live, as you know, next door. You must stay with us until your father returns.'

'But surely he won't be gone long,' Selma exclaimed.

'The Professor Bey is unpredictable,' Ahmet remarked evasively. 'If you will follow me.'

He picked up the two heavier cases, and Venice took the lighter ones; Selma carried nothing except the magazines they had bought to read on the journey and her handbag. She walked beside Ahmet, leaving Venice to trudge in their rear. He probably thought she was some sort of maid–companion, Venice reflected with amusement, and perhaps in a sense she was.

The villa was divided from its neighbour by a high brick wall in which was an arched doorway, but no door. If there had once been one it had been removed; the path leading to it was well worn; evidently commerce between the two establishments was frequent.

The Osman abode stood higher up the rise, overlooking the road, and the Bosphorus beyond it. The front had been refaced in white stone and looked modern, but the back was as it had originally been, an old Ottoman mansion built mostly of wood. It looked on to a large walled courtyard, in which was a fountain. Beyond the high surround was a line of cypresses, excluding it from the hillside. It was into this yard that Ahmet led them. An upstairs gallery ran the length of the house, supported by pillars which formed a shaded arcade beneath it, which was furnished with canvas chairs, loungers and wrought iron tables painted white. Wisteria and a vine climbed the pillars, but were pruned short in front of the gallery windows, which were covered with latticework. There were tubs of flowers dotted about the courtyard, mostly filled with geraniums which gave colour to the scene. In one corner was a dovecote, from which came a perpetual cooing as its inmates preened themselves on its roof. It was a secluded and pleasant spot in which apparently the family did most of its living in fine weather.

Ahmet indicated the chairs in the arcade:

'You will sit and rest, yes? The drinks will be brought to you.' He was eyeing Selma's striking garb appreciatively; it showed off her well rounded limbs. Venice recalled that Turks were supposed to admire curves and reflected that her own slim boyish figure was unlikely to be admired, which was as well from Bill's point of view. Ahmet was quite devastatingly handsome. Not that she was likely to allow her fancy to stray in the direction of a foreigner, but it was a little trying to be so completely ignored. Ahmet went on:

'Later you will be shown to your rooms, and ...' the dark eyes crinkled in mirth, 'have the bath.'

'But we can't stay here,' Selma objected.

'For the present, yes,' he said firmly. 'Until the Professor Bey ... returns.' He paused before the last word, and again Venice felt the chill of apprehension. She was much more sensitive to nuances than her friend and she was vaguely aware that something was wrong.

'It is not good that two young ladies are in a house alone,' Ahmet declared. He picked up two of the cases. 'Ismael will bring the rest of your luggage. Meanwhile, please to sit.'

He departed into the house, leaving the two girls to stare at each other in dismay.

'Well, what do you make of that?' Selma asked.

'It would seem your father is away from home and is not expected back immediately,' Venice replied.

'Well, really, I'll have something to say when he does turn up,' Selma said emphatically. 'He over plays the absent-minded Professor to an unpardonable degree.'

'If he really has forgotten ...' Venice began, and stopped. No need to frighten Selma with her vague fears. She did not believe Lucas Hadleigh had forgotten they were coming and Ahmet had expected them. Possibly he had been called away upon some important business and had asked the Osmans to look after them. But there was no need for them to stay with them, surely? There was a perfectly good house next door where they could fend for themselves.

'Of course he has,' Selma said testily. She had sat down on the most comfortable lounger and pulled off her hat. She began to look pensive.

'Ahmet has grown into quite something,' she observed, and giggled. 'I don't think I'm going to be bored!'

A girl came out carrying a tray upon which were two tall glasses of iced fruit juice. She was short and plump with a round face and flat features. Although dressed in a nondescript skirt and blouse, she had a piece of drapery over her head, which upon the approach of a strange male she would instinctively draw over the lower part of her face. Old customs die hard among the peasantry. She was followed by a slim dark boy in jeans and tee-shirt who grabbed their remaining gear and vanished indoors. The girl offered the glasses with a shy smile, saying something they did not understand. Selma seized one with avidity, and Venice took the other, sitting down on one of the iron chairs. The girl smiled again and withdrew.

'Ah, that's better,' Selma sighed, after taking a deep draught. She lay back in her seat. 'Why don't you make yourself comfortable, Ven?'

'Because I don't feel comfortable,' Venice said. 'These people are complete strangers to me. They may be your kin, but they'll regard me as an interloper.'

'Don't be absurd, Ven. Turks are famed for their hospitality. To them you're a guest, and they'll do anything for you. Until we discover what's happened to Pa, we'll have to take things as they come, and I for one find this place delightful.' She stretched her slim body on the lounger and closed her eyes.

Venice sipped her drink reflectively. Selma was right —they could do nothing until they obtained more information. Perhaps the Professor had left a message with someone and it would be delivered to them later. The traffic from the road was only a muted distant sound in this quiet retreat, the murmur of the doves was much louder. Golden afternoon sunshine filled the courtyard, which seemed to belong to another and more distant age. Difficult to realise that it was only that morning that she had said goodbye to Bill in England.

The whisper of a sandal on stone caused her to look round, and she saw that a second young man had come out into the arcade. He was standing behind her surveying Selma's recumbent figure with a slight frown. Thus she was able to survey him without his knowledge. She surmised this must be the other brother, Kemal, but they were not much alike. He was shorter than the other man, not nearly so good-looking, more fair than dark, and except for a good breadth of shoulder, he was very slight. But he would never be overlooked, for his whole being was vibrant with whipcord energy. A man who obviously lived on his nerves, there was not an ounce of surplus flesh on his lean body, and the thin sun-tanned face was set in strong, almost austere lines. Even in that first glimpse of him, Venice was aware of his forceful personality. He was casually dressed in slacks and a tee-shirt, which contrasted with his brother's elegant suit, but he had something that made other handsomer and taller men seem insignificant.

Becoming aware of her gaze, he turned his head and their eyes met. His, she saw, were steel grey and penetrating; he seemed to probe past her outer seeming deep into her hidden thoughts. Involuntarily it occurred to her that he would be a difficult man to deceive.

His thin mouth twisted into a wry smile, and he looked again at Selma.

'You are very welcome, but which of you is my cousin?' His voice was surprisingly deep and resonant.

As she remembered Professor Hadleigh's plans, Venice's smile was equally wry. Surprising that he did not recognise Selma, but girls change when they become grown up, even to the colour of their hair. He must be wondering which was the intended bride, the beauty dozing in the canvas lounger or her far more insignificant self. She recalled also that there had been no indication which was the favourite for Selma's hand; possibly she was to make her choice, in which case Ahmet would have had a head start.

'She is Selma Hadleigh,' she indicated the girl on

31

the lounger. 'Don't you remember her?'

'She was only a schoolgirl when I saw her last.' He eyed the black trousers with distaste. 'You are her chaperone?'

Venice laughed. 'Do I look so old?'

He moved round to face her.

'On the contrary, a mere infant.' And this time his smile was wholly charming, lighting up the severe planes of his face.

'Rather more than that. I'm what they used to call in old plays the confidant.'

'Meaning you receive your friend's secrets?'

She found his keen grey gaze a little disconcerting, but she met it unwaveringly.

'Some of them,' she admitted, 'but no woman ever tells another everything.'

'Women are devious creatures.'

'I flatter myself I'm very straightforward.'

'Then you're an exception.' He sat down astride another high chair opposite to her. He had less accent than his brother and he continued to stare at her.

'You have most strange eyes,' he exclaimed, 'like green fire. And you are not afraid to return a man's gaze.'

'Oh, really!' Venice blushed faintly and turned her head away. The faint colour became her, illuminating her delicate features. Her fair hair, released from her hat, curled softly about her well shaped head and framed the entrancing lines of face and throat. Though Selma usually put her in the shade, Venice's appearance had a subtle charm that was not at first glance apparent.

'Forgive me,' he said apologetically. 'That was not polite. You see, in your country women were never put in purdah. Here even now they shrink from men's eyes, except the most modern ones. No wonder if in the old days they became devious—they could only attain their ends by the use of subtlety. The seraglios were hotbeds of feminine intrigue, and many a sultan met his end by reason of them.'

Venice turned her head to meet his keen regard again, unable to resist this challenge and show she was not afraid. Her eyes glinted mischievously as she asked demurely:

'Do you regret those days when women were utterly subservient to their masters' will?'

'Certainly not. The Ghazi,' he inclined his head in reverence, 'had the right idea when he declared women should be man's equal in defiance of Islam's teaching. Should I consider my mother to be inferior to my father?'

'It must have been a great innovation for Turkey,' Venice said reflectively, recollecting how the revolution had changed the country. The Ghazi was one of the titles given to Ataturk, the dictator who had inaugurated the metamorphosis.

'It was. Oddly enough, women were very reluctant to discard the veil. Some in the country still wear it.'

'Force of habit,' Venice suggested.

'Perhaps—but I am most remiss. How did we come to embark upon such a subject? You are a guest, and I do not even know your name.'

'Venice Franklin.'

'Venice? But that is a place name.'

'So is Florence, and that's also a girl's name. My mother had her reasons for choosing it. You of course are one of the Mr Osmans?'

'Kemal—I was named for a very great man. Please to call me that.'

Venice remembered what Selma had told her. First names were the custom here, so she could not object.

'Kemal!' Selma had woken up. 'You must be Kemal,

as the other one's Ahmet.' She gave her sexy chuckle and held out her hand. 'Am I welcome, dear cousin?'

Kemal had sprung to his feet when she spoke. He went swiftly towards her, but he merely touched her fingertips.

'Most welcome, Selma Hanim.'

Venice was surprised by the warmth of Selma's greeting, which was much more so than the one she had given Ahmet, but then she had been cross and tired. Now she was rested and her great eyes were fixed upon the young man with that languorous appeal that promised everything and meant nothing.

'Perhaps you'll tell me what's happened to Pa,' she went on. 'Ahmet brought us over here and talked about us staying here, which is all nonsense, because he'll be back soon, won't he?'

Kemal was silent as if considering his words, and again Venice felt a dart of apprehension. Then he said quietly:

'That we do not know.'

Selma sat up abruptly. 'Don't know? What do you mean? Where's he gone?'

'I wish we could tell you that. I am afraid, dear cousin, we have distressing news for you. Yesterday the Professor Bey disappeared, and we do not know what has become of him.'

But Selma attached no great importance to this announcement, being used to her father's erratic ways.

'He really is the limit!' she exclaimed. 'I suppose someone mentioned some old ruin and he rushed off to inspect it, leaving us in the lurch.'

A silence followed her words. Glancing at Kemal's face, Venice was sure he did not accept Selma's explanation. Presently he said carefully:

'I am sure your father would not overlook your arrival. He was looking forward to it.'

'You don't know him as well as I do,' Selma flashed. 'A daughter can't compete with a relic that's a thousand years old.'

Kemal frowned at her levity. 'I do know him very well,' he corrected her. 'He is never discourteous.' He moved over to the fountain and staring at the spray of water added: 'Perhaps I should tell you that the Professor Bey hired a motor boat and was seen travelling up the Bosphorus towards the Kara Deniz. He did not return.'

Venice asked anxiously, 'You think he met with an accident?'

'There has been no report of one, nor has anybody seen him or the boat since. If he had reached the Black Sea and was forced to land, he may be in a Communist country.' He looked significantly at Selma, but she only laughed.

'Then why make such heavy weather about it? If he did, there'll be a delay in letting you know his whereabouts, won't there?'

'That may be so,' he agreed, half relieved, half irritated that she had missed his point.

'Was he alone?' Venice enquired.

'Yes, and if his engine failed, I fear he was not very good as a mechanic.'

'The world's worst,' Selma corroborated. She looked from one to the other of their serious faces, and then something of the anxiety both were trying to suppress communicated itself to her. She sprang up from her seat, her façade of indifference collapsing, and flung herself into Kemal's arms, her beautiful face contorted with grief.

'Cousin . . . cousin, you don't think he's drowned?'

She lifted her lovely eyes to his face, from which tears had begun to drip. Venice moved uncomfortably, assailed by the unworthy suspicion that this exhibition was caused less by anxiety for her father than a desire to impress Kemal, who seemed to expect her to be upset; it was also an opportunity to flaunt her femininity. Selma could never resist trying to attract a personable male.

Though he looked a little embarrassed, Kemal was quite equal to this display of emotion. He put a brotherly arm around her, and stroked her hair soothingly with his free hand. To Venice the spectacle was a little repellant, she could not imagine why, unless it was because she doubted Selma's sincerity; neither of the Osman brothers was of the slightest interest to her.

'Do not give up hope,' he told Selma gently in his precise English. 'Quite likely he has been picked up by some passing craft.'

At that moment Ahmet came strolling out into the arcade. Venice saw him raise his brows as he saw his brother apparently embracing their guest. She said quickly:

'Your brother has been telling Selma that the Professor is apparently lost at sea, and it naturally came as a shock to her.'

'Oh, I am sure he will have been rescued,' Ahmet said easily. 'Kem is an alarmist.' He shot the other man a venomous glance. 'Though it seems to pay dividends. He is privileged to have the pleasure of comforting her.'

Oh dear, Venice thought, are they going to quarrel over Selma's favours? She knew that was a situation her frivolous friend would enjoy, but in dealing with men of another nationality it might be dangerous. Apart from the possibility of arousing Oriental passions it would be most inconvenient to cause dissention in their host's family, since they seemed to be their only friends in an awkward predicament.

Kemal had dropped his arm when Ahmet spoke, and

now he gently pushed Selma away from him. She gave him a seductive smile and turned her attention to Ahmet.

'You must forgive me,' she said sweetly, 'but Kem's news gave me a shock. There,' she wiped her eyes, 'I'm all right now.'

'My mother wishes to receive you,' Ahmet told her formally. 'She is something of an invalid and seldom leaves her room since her husband's sudden death. Will you come this way?' As an afterthought, he added: 'And you also, Venice Hanim.' Somebody must have told him her name.

'Certainly, Ahmet Bey,' Selma emphasised the Bey provocatively. 'But we modern young people have dispensed with formalities.' She gave each young man a brilliant smile. 'Lead on, Macduff.'

Ahmet raised an eyebrow. 'Macduff? I do not know him.'

'A quotation from Shakespeare,' Venice explained.

'Ah yes, your great bard. Kem will know him, I am not so well educated in English literature.' Again a barbed glance.

'Actually it should be "*lay* on, Macduff",' Kemal said stiffly. 'I will see you later.'

Venice followed Selma aware of antagonism between the brothers, or were they half-brothers? Ahmet had said 'my mother,' so she might not be Kemal's. Turks could have three wives according to the Koran, or was it four? Though Selma had told her that monogamy was now the rule. This was a strange household and she wished heartily that they could go back to Villa Yasmin and be independent.

Ahmet followed them down a dim cool passage until they came to a staircase, and he indicated that they should ascend it. At the top of it he ushered them into a room that could have come out of The Arabian

Nights. The floor was covered by thick carpeting, seats covered with cushions ran round three sides of the room. Small inlaid tables were dotted about at intervals. Shutters of green latticework covered the windows which overlooked the courtyard. The sun penetrated through the open work, strewing the room with shining lozenges of gold. On the wide seat beneath the window a woman was reclining, wearing a caftan, her dark hair loose over her shoulders beneath a flimsy veil. Round her neck she wore a heavy gold necklace, and bracelets adorned her wrists. Beside her on a low table were cigarettes, an ornate ash tray, and a box of sweets. In addition, striking an incongruous note, was a pile of Western magazines, including French and English ones.

As the girls came in she did not rise but smiled at them in a friendly manner. Venice noticed that Ahmet was very like her, the same regular features and fine dark eyes. Undoubtedly she was *his* mother.

'Come and sit beside me,' she said in English, indicating the divan stretching on either side of her. 'Ahmet, bid Aziza bring ...' She looked at them interrogatively. 'Tea or coffee? The English drink tea at this hour, do they not?'

Venice, doubtful as to what Turkish tea would be like, hesitated, but Selma, who knew what to expect, said she would love a glass of tea. 'It comes with lemon and no milk,' she informed her friend.

'If you please, Ahmet,' said his mother. He inclined his head and withdrew.

'You will pardon me for not coming down to meet you,' their hostess went on, as the girls seated themselves one on each side of her. 'I am not strong and always I rest in the afternoon. I hope my son made you welcome?'

'He did his best,' Selma told her, dimpling.

The woman was studying her closely. 'You have grown very lovely, Selma,' she said.'

Selma smiled. 'Thank you, Zubeyde Hanim,' she returned. 'I was just at the awkward age when you saw me last, wasn't I? But this is my friend Venice,' she indicated Venice. 'She has come to keep me company.'

'It is well,' Zubeyde approved. 'A young girl should not go about alone. Ahmet has told you our sad news?'

'Kem did.'

'Ah, Kem. He is not my son, but being the elder he takes his father's place as head of the household.'

Venice wondered if her husband had had two wives, and noticing her expression, Zubeyde laughed. 'My husband was a widower when he married me. Ataturk decreed that a man should only have one wife at a time, as in your country. We are very Western in our ways now. Ah, here is Aziza with the tea.'

The same maid who had brought them the iced drinks came in with a tray. She set it down and brought another table within her mistress's reach to put it upon. The tea was in tall glasses with, as Selma had said, a slice of lemon; there was a sugar basin and a plate of biscuits. Aziza made some remark in Turkish, made a sketch of a salaam and went away. The tea was quite a different drink from an English 'cuppa', but it was very refreshing; the biscuits, Venice was amused to see, were an English brand.

Their hostess told them: 'We have every hope that the Professor Bey will soon be found, but until he is with us again you may stay here. I have ordered rooms to be prepared for you.'

Both Selma and Venice protested, saying they could not impose upon her hospitality and they could manage perfectly well on their own in the house next door.

'It is not to be heard of.' Zubeyde Hanim was emphatic. 'You may be British and independent, but I

cannot allow you to be a scandal among our friends.'
She smiled winningly. 'Will you deny us the pleasure
of entertaining our esteemed neighbour's daughters ...
daughter?' she corrected herself. 'Besides, I am told his
servants have gone home.'

'In that case we'll be glad to stay with you,' Selma declared. She did not like doing domestic chores. 'You are
very kind, Zubeyde Hanim.'

Venice did not at all want to accept this offer, already
she had sensed tension in the air where Selma was concerned, but she could not object further since Selma
had agreed.

'Your baggage will be in your rooms,' Zubeyde told
them. 'And I will ring for Aziza to show you to them.
We have dinner downstairs at eight o'clock in the
European manner, and I will come down to chaperone
you.' She sighed. 'My son insists, as did my dear
husband, that we are modern and must adapt to
Western ways, but sometimes I feel it is a mistake, and
I feel the old ways were best.'

Selma stared at her in horror. 'But then you would
be shut up in a seraglio!'

'I should have been sheltered and protected,'
Zubeyde pointed out. 'Freedom has its price. You, my
dear, would be discreetly veiled until the time came to
present you to your husband. It saved ... complica-
tions.'

She's no fool, Venice thought; she's afraid as I am
that Selma may engender jealousy between her son and
his brother. I wonder if they've decided among themselves which one should marry her. That is if she con-
sents to take either of them.

Selma was looking wicked and Venice was uneasily
aware that she meant to exploit the situation. In response to Zubeyde's remarks, she said demurely:

'Women nowadays have other things to think about besides marriage.'

'I am told you have the good education, yes, yes?' the Turkish woman queried, eyeing her thoughtfully. 'That seems to me to be a waste of energy, for surely marriage is your goal. I am told women pursue careers even after they are wed. Kem is very insistent that women should be equal with men, but a woman's home and children should be sufficient occupation for her.' She shook her dark head regretfully. 'I cannot understand the modern viewpoint.'

'Regular old diehard, isn't she?' Selma observed when Aziza had been summoned and shown them to their rooms. 'She's afraid I'll demoralise her precious son!'

She was in Venice's room and she looked round it appreciatively. Both it and her own next door—they were connected by a bathroom with doors into each—were comfortably furnished with Western style furniture and divan beds, though the wardrobes and dressers were a little on the heavy side. The windows looked over the courtyard, and were fitted with Venetian blinds, drawn against the heat of the sun.

'I think we're better off here than we'd be in the villa,' Selma went on, 'and I'm much too tired to want to bother with preparing a meal. There was no need for you to go on about being an imposition. They like having visitors, and I think it'll be fun staying here.'

She sat down on Venice's bed, an impish smile curving her lips, looking like a young witch brooding over her spells.

'Do be careful,' Venice besought her. 'You aren't dealing with Englishmen, you know.'

'Men are the same whatever their nationality,' Selma returned. 'They all have passions. My cousin Ahmet is certainly a dish, but how can I marry him unless I dis-

41

cover what makes him tick? Those ancient marriages must have been terrible, not knowing what your bridegroom looked like until after you were tied to him, though I bet those girls managed to get a peek at him beforehand, but it was buying a pig in a poke.'

Venice was inexplicably relieved that Selma's sights were set upon the younger man. It could not matter to her which one she chose.

'You don't seem very anxious about your father,' she said reproachfully.

'Of course I am, but there's no use brooding about it,' Selma returned. 'He's probably landed somewhere along the coast and will turn up at any moment, and we're very foolish to worry about him.'

Venice was glad that Selma persisted in her optimism, and she supposed she might be right, though Kemal had said they had already searched and made enquiries without a clue. She went to the window and pulled up the blind so that she could look outside. The sun was setting and the evening air was cooler. She drew back hastily as she saw Kemal pacing the tiled paving. He had already changed for the evening meal and was wearing a white jacket over dark trousers, a garb that suited his slender but muscular figure. He moved with feline grace, his brows knitted in thought. His intense physical magnetism seem to reach even to where she stood regarding him.

'What is it?' Selma asked, coming to stand beside her. 'Oh, cousin Kem. Looks nice in that rig-out, but something seems to be biting him.'

'Perhaps he's thinking about your father.'

'Not him, Pa's not important enough,' Selma declared. 'Kem's always concerned with the fate of the nation, or perhaps he merely wants his dinner, and that's why he's prowling like a hungry lion. Just shows he can't believe Pa's in any real danger or he'd be out looking for him.'

Venice had rather deplored Selma's easy acceptance of her father's predicament, but she was sure Kemal was anxious about him.

'Since he's already searched he can only wait to receive news of him from local sources,' she suggested.

'Maybe he's had a hand in it himself,' Selma observed flippantly. 'He looks a ruthless type.'

'But why on earth?'

Selma moved away from the window and struck a dramatic pose.

'A lever to win my consent to his fell purposes,' she declaimed. 'Marry me and hand over your dowry and I'll produce your dad. Refuse me and you'll never see him again.'

'Selma, you're being absurd! He's a civilised person.'

'Of course I am,' Selma laughed, 'but the civilisation is only skin-deep. As you keep warning me, they're not men to play with, they haven't completely subdued the original Ottoman, and they could and did act like savages upon occasion.' As Venice looked sceptical, she added seriously:

'My mother was one of them, so I should know.'

CHAPTER THREE

SELMA chose to wear for dinner a long silk gown of a bright orange shade that left her arms and shoulders bare. She draped over her décolletée a magnificent black and gold stole. She took from her case a collar of gold segments interspersed with topaz which looked Egyptian. Her hair she coiled about her head and she put on long gold ear-rings. The total effect was very un-English and Venice thought she had never seen Selma look more beautiful or more barbaric. Her own long dress of flowered printed nylon looked juvenile and uninteresting against such splendour. It had discreet cap sleeves, and modest neckline. About her neck she clasped a blue enamel pendant on a silver chain, a gift from Bill.

Selma completely eclipsed her, but that was as it should be, she reflected as she fastened her silver sandals; she was in the position of a poor dependant who had come along to lend her friend countenance and it behoved her to appear inconspicuous. What she did not suspect was that amidst the oriental furnishings of the house, and contrasted with Selma's and Zubeyde's exotic beauty, for their hostess was still a very handsome woman, her Anglo-Saxon features and simple clothes stood out in almost startling vividness. They blended with the mosaic patterns on the walls, the rich hangings and ornate inlaid furniture. But she was like a white narcissus between a pair of brilliant red peonies. When she was seated at the dinner table, at which Zubeyde sat at the head and Kemal opposite to her, with Selma and Ahmet facing her, she had all the charm of novelty for the two young men who were both silently appraising her, while Zubeyde backed up by Selma dominated the conversation.

The dining room and sitting room were at the back of the house, their windows opening on to the arcade, and as they never got direct sunlight were always cool. Ismael waited upon them in what looked like a white Eton suit with its short jacket.

The meal was served in the Western manner, though the food was unfamiliar, starting with a baked fish of some unknown variety from the Bosphorus with a rich sauce, followed by spiced lamb and rice. The sweet was a concoction of honey and almond paste flavoured with pistachio nuts. There was also fresh fruit in abundance and French wine. At its conclusion, Zubeyde told Ismael they would take coffee in the arcade. Her dress was satin heavily embroidered with long full sleeves which somehow managed to look oriental, although it was a Paris model. Throughout the meal none of them had mentioned the subject that must have been uppermost in their minds, but as she passed Kemal on her way outside, Venice asked in an undertone:

'Is there still no news?'

He shook his head. 'Morning will perhaps bring light,' he said with Eastern ambiguity.

Low as she had spoken, Selma heard her.

'He must have landed somewhere along the coast,' she said irritably. 'He'll turn up full of apologies saying he was on the track of some old ruin and forgot all about us.'

'I am sure I hope that will prove so,' Kemal said gravely. 'So do not allow anxiety to disturb your rest.' But Venice noticed he exchanged a meaning glance with his brother.

'Oh, if I worried over Pa's disappearances I'd be grey-haired by now,' Selma spoke cheerfully. 'What do you do in the evenings here when you don't go out? Have you a television?'

'No. There is television in Istanbul, but the reception here is erratic,' Ahmet told her. 'We have, though, a radio.'

'Lead me to it.'

She went indoors with Ahmet, and Zubeyde made a half movement to follow them, but Kemal restrained her.

'Let them go. Selma is Western and will resent a chaperone.'

Zubeyde subsided with a sigh. 'New times, new manners.'

'Precisely,' Kemal agreed. He turned to Venice and explained that in that country it was still considered compromising for a woman to go out alone with a man.

'But Selma is still in the house,' Venice pointed out.

'For tonight, yes, but she will not be content to remain so for long. We shall have trouble with that one, I think, she is too beautiful to be unguarded.'

Venice felt suddenly depressed. It was sometimes a little trying to be the ugly duckling and she was sure Kemal would not consider that she needed a guardian. She stood up, a slim reed of a girl, her dress palely gleaming in the shadowed arcade.

'If you'll excuse me, I'd like to go to bed. I'm very tired. No, don't disturb yourselves,' as Kemal sprang to his feet and Zubeyde moved in her chair, 'I can find my way. Goodnight.'

They both bade her a good night and pleasant dreams, Kemal adding mischievously: '*Karin gorusuruz.*'

'What on earth does that mean?' she asked.

'Until tomorrow.'

Incomprehensible language, she thought as she

wended her way to her room. Until tomorrow? What would the morrow bring forth?

She was in bed but not asleep when Selma came up. Having ascertained that Venice was awake, Selma came to sit upon her bed and talk, as she had so often done in the past when they had shared their girlish confidences. With her long hair loose upon her shoulders, wearing a brocade wrap over her nightdress, she looked more Eastern than English; since she had come to Turkey her heritage from her mother had come to the fore. She had used her time with Ahmet to pump him about the family's affairs.

'It's only fair I should know their circumstances,' she said with a sly look.

It appeared they owned the house in which they lived and had another property in Ankara where Kemal would be going to live as he had been elected to the National Assembly, but most of their money was invested in tourism, which though a government concern needed private capital to expand. Kemal was manager of an office in Istanbul, but was at present on sick leave after a bout of fever.

'Very earnest person, Cousin Kem,' Selma said a little scornfully. Ahmet, she went on, was much younger than his brother and shared her determination to get fun out of life. He had just completed his two years' compulsory service in the Army which every young Turk had to do when he was twenty and was undecided whether to take over Kem's position when his brother left for Ankara or apply for a long-term commission and return to the Army.

'I told him to do that,' Selma said. 'Soldiers are so much more romantic than business men, but he suggested it might not be the sort of life that would appeal to his wife.'

'Is he engaged, then?' Venice asked with pretended innocence.

'Of course not, you nut! He was looking at me when he said it. He's got beautiful eyes and he knows how to use them. When he fixes them on me I go all gooey.'

'Doubtless you aren't the only one so affected,' Venice warned her drily.

'I wouldn't want an inexperienced man,' Selma declared, 'and I'll admit Ahmet may be a bit of a philanderer, if they do philander in this country. That makes him all the more exciting.'

Venice reflected that Ahmet had very successfully distracted Selma from worrying about her father. As if sensing her thought, Selma said defensively:

'You think I'm heartless, don't you? But I'm sure Pa'll turn up okay. The fact that he went out at all indicates that he had some object in view. He was never one for taking little trips just for pleasure.'

Though she liked to dramatise every situation that arose, Selma's histrionics were entirely superficial and she was always optimistic. Venice wished she possessed her sanguine temperament, she herself was deeply troubled about her old friend's disappearance and was sure Kemal was too. However, she did not wish to disturb Selma's confidence even if it were misplaced, and finally her friend left her to go to her own room, doubtless to dream of Ahmet's fine eyes.

Venice passed a restless night; too much had happened on the previous day and she was over-stimulated. When she dozed it was not Ahmet's fine eyes that haunted her dreams, but Kemal's keen grey ones. The man intrigued her, but she did not want to think about him. Resolutely she tried to concentrate upon Bill, who would be travelling north to his mountains, but he seemed to be very far away. Finally, when it was fully daylight, she got up. She looked in at Selma and found her peacefully sleeping, then took a shower in their joint bathroom. The mirror above the basin reflected a pale face with mauve shadows beneath her eyes, the result of lack of sleep and fatigue; even her hair looked lustreless. Upon returning to her room she brushed it hard, and after applying some make-up she managed to remove the worst traces of her uneasy night. She put on a pair of light trousers and a tank top, hoping that such a dress would not offend any Turkish susceptibilities. She had been assured that Miss Modern Turkey followed the fashions, but she thought Zubeyde would not approve, though after all, the original native costume had included trousers, though of a much more voluminous style.

She encountered no one as she went downstairs and out into the courtyard. The sun was rising and a mist hung over the water and hills, blocked from her view by the high walls, but the air was fresh and cool scented by a summer jasmine draping one of the walls. The doves had left their cote and were strutting round the edge of the fountain, neutral-tinted Barbarys with black neck rings and speckled turtle-doves, their amorous cooing accompanying the faint splash of the falling water from the fountain. It was very quiet; the traffic ran by on the other side of the house, its noise muted by the intervening building, but it had not yet begun to flow.

At first Venice thought she was alone, until a slim figure detached itself from the shadow cast by the wall and she saw that it was Kemal.

'Good morning,' he called as he came towards her. 'You are up very early.'

She returned his greeting, adding: 'When it's hot the early morning is the pleasantest time.'

The doves rose with a whirl of wings as he came up to her. Venice, to her surprise, felt suddenly shy. There

49

was something very attractive about this virile young man with his thin brown face and penetrating grey eyes that drew her in spite of herself. She was all at once conscious of her womanhood in a way that Bill had never been able to make her feel.

'I suppose you haven't heard anything?' she asked, looking down at the paving stones on which she stood.

He shook his smooth brown head on which the hair was cut short.

'I am afraid not.' He hesitated, then told her, 'I would not say this to Selma, I do not wish to alarm her, but you seem to be a sensible girl who will not weep on my shoulder.' He smiled wryly, recalling Selma's behaviour. 'It occurs to me that this disappearance may not be an accident. Hadleigh Bey is an eminent scientist, and he was heading towards the Black Sea which the Russians consider to be their sea, though we dispute that. He may have been ... intercepted.'

'Do you mean kidnapped?' Venice asked bluntly. 'I don't think that's likely, he wasn't all that famous.'

'They might find him ... useful,' Kemal said.

Although the sun was gaining strength, Venice felt suddenly cold. All the stories she had read upon this theme recurred to her with unpleasant force. She had forgotten the close proximity of the Soviet territories, and she looked at Kemal in dismay.

'But ... in that case ... will we ever hear of him again?' she asked faintly.

'Oh, sure to,' he returned quickly. 'Though perhaps not for some time. Although the Communist countries are not exactly communicative it is possible to make enquiries, and I am arranging to do so. There are ships going daily to Odessa and the Crimea, and we have agents.'

Venice sat down abruptly on the stone rim of the fountain.

'One reads about this sort of thing,' she said quietly. 'But it never seems real. I still can't think Professor Hadleigh is important enough to be kidnapped. He's been retired for some years and his knowledge must be getting a bit out of date.'

'That was your word, not mine,' Kemal insisted gently. 'He may have been picked up if his boat was out of control, and is merely being held ... temporarily. This is only supposition, so please do not mention it to Selma. We must continue to try to keep her ... what do you say ... in the paradise of fools until we are more certain.' He smiled mischievously. 'Ahmet will continue to distract her.'

Venice was aware of a faint resentment. Kemal had confided in her because he considered she was sensible and unlikely to embarrass him by a display of panic while Selma must be shielded and protected from harsh realities. True, the Professor was her father, not Venice's, and naturally Selma would be expected to be more concerned about his fate than herself, but it was more fundamental than that. Instinctively she knew that Selma's femininity had aroused Kemal's protective urges, while she was only her companion to be recruited into his campaign to lull Selma's fears, and he probably did not see her as a woman at all in her boyish garb. She said reproachfully:

'I think a lot of Professor Hadleigh. It would grieve me very much if anything has happened to him.'

'So it would us all,' Kemal assured her.

'But you think I'm tougher than Selma?'

'Tough?' The word as applied to herself seemed to puzzle him.

'Oh, forget it.' She became ashamed of her moment's pique. His opinion of her did not matter in the least and naturally his consideration was all for Selma, who was his kin and might become something much closer. 'Thank you for telling me,' she went on with a sweet smile that gave her a fleeting elusive beauty, 'but don't you think Selma might prefer to think her father is in Soviet hands than to believe he's drowned?'

Kemal looked startled. 'Does she believe he's drowned?'

Remembering Selma's peacefully sleeping face, Venice shook her head. 'Not yet, but she may get round to it.'

'Then we must keep her hopes alive,' he said absently, seeming diverted by some new thought.

'I'm with you there,' Venice assured him, and became aware that he was studying her with a quizzical look in his eyes. Thinking perhaps her appearance displeased him, she said quickly:

'I hope your mother ...' then she remembered Zubeyde was not his mother and corrected herself stumbling over the unfamiliar words, 'I mean Zubeyde H ... Hanim doesn't object to women wearing trousers.'

'Zubeyde must accustom herself to Western dress,' he declared harshly, not denying that she might disapprove. 'We are in the twentieth century now. The great Ataturk dispensed with the fez and the veil, making many other innovations, and we owe it to his memory to continue to advance.'

His face glowed when he spoke of the dead dictator and his eyes shone with the light of hero-worship; almost he seemed to increase in stature. Venice gazed at him in wonder; she did not know much Turkish history, ancient or modern, and it seemed extraordinary to her that a man who must have died before he was born could arouse such emotion in the self-contained man before her. Involuntarily she thought it would be a fortunate woman who could bring such a change to his rather severe face and he would be a wonderful lover.

'It is my great regret,' he went on, his eyes fixed on the hillside above the wall as if he saw a vision, 'that I came into the world too late to know him and to serve him.'

Venice became irritated, the woman in her subconsciously jealous of this adoration of his hero.

'I might say the same about Florence Nightingale,' she said flippantly. 'She was an exceptional woman, but her service must have been very uncomfortable.'

'Nursing!' he exclaimed scornfully. 'Kemal Ataturk created a vigorous modern nation out of the degenerate remains of the Ottoman Empire. There is no comparison.' Then he seemed to recollect to whom he was speaking, the light died out of his eyes as he brought his regard back to her. 'But I cannot expect you to share my enthusiasm,' he said apologetically. 'And I am keeping you from your breakfast, while I bore you with my eulogies.'

'I'm not bored,' she returned. 'I don't know much about Turkey. I'd like to learn more.'

He gave her a wary glance as if doubtful of her sincerity.

'There are books,' he said stiffly.

'So there are,' she agreed brightly. 'Perhaps you'll lend me some, especially one about your hero.'

He smiled at her eagerness. 'If you wish, but it is a dull subject for a vacation.'

A shadow crossed her mobile face as she recalled her missing host.

'It won't be much of a holiday unless the Professor is found.'

'Allah grant he may soon be so,' Kemal ejaculated piously, and his phrase reminded Venice of the great gulf between them that she had almost forgotten. He was alien in every possible way from herself.

'Here is Aziza with the breakfast,' he went on as the maid appeared carrying a tray, 'and also Selma.'

He went swiftly towards Selma who had come out into the courtyard as if he were relieved by the interruption. Unlike Venice, Selma had put on a dress, pink linen, that suited her dark colouring, and she made an entrancing picture standing in front of the pillars of the arcade. As Kemal approached her she gave him a slow seductive smile. Venice followed slowly; she had noted the alacrity with which Kemal had left her to go to Selma and had to repress a faint stab of jealousy. She was perfectly indifferent towards Kem Osman and all his doings. Later in the day she must remember to write to Bill, but she was not sure what to say about Professor Hadleigh or her future plans. If he did not turn up she could hardly spend her whole holiday imposing on the Osmans.

Breakfast apparently was in summer always served in the arcade and Zubeyde did not come down to it. Aziza brought fresh rolls, coffee with milk, not the thick sweet stuff they had after dinner, butter, honey and fruit. The doves gathered round them hoping for crumbs. One flew up on to the arm of Venice's chair and took a piece of roll from her fingers. It was mauve and grey with black spots, and eyes like rubies. They made a charming picture.

'Take care it doesn't mess your dress,' Selma warned rather spitefully; she had noticed her companions' appreciative looks and she did not like birds.

Kemal announced that he had to go into Istanbul and suggested they should accompany him and Ahmet could show them the town while he did his business. Selma pouted.

'I thought you were on sick leave, Kem.'

'So I am, but there are still affairs upon which I wish to ... what do you say ... keep an eye?'

'That's right. Your English is very good—and yours.' She smiled at Ahmet. 'Where did you learn it?'

'At school, and Kem has been to England,' Ahmet told her. 'We also had to learn French and German. Istanbul is cosmopolitan, as you know, so we have much practice in the city, and few visitors know Turkish.' He threw a malicious glance at his brother. 'Especially the new Turkish.'

'New?' Venice was puzzled. 'Is it a different language?'

'No, but my brother's hero tried to purify it, throwing out the Arabic and Greek words when the Latinised the script. It led to some confusion, and now a lot of the old words are creeping back. Actually Kemal should be Kamal in Turkish.'

This was too like a lesson for Selma, who shrugged her shoulders impatiently. 'Don't suppose I'll ever learn it,' she said. 'And I prefer Kem to Kam.' She smiled at the bearer of that name.

'Kemal means perfection,' Ahmet informed her, seeming intent upon needling his brother. 'And you will find him very difficult to please.'

'I am not a perfectionist,' Kem declared, 'I only aspire to be a loyal to my country.'

'I'm sure you are,' Selma yawned. 'When do we start?'

'As soon as we have finished breakfast,' Kem told her. 'It will be very hot.' He looked doubtfully at Venice.

'Then I'll change into a dress,' she said, interpreting his expression correctly, 'but don't all the tourists wear trousers?'

'You are not a tourist,' he pointed out, 'but a guest of the Osmans.'

'Who are something in the city?' she asked pertly.

'Precisely.'

'Oh, Ven won't disgrace you,' Selma said indolently. 'She's got a lot of suitable dresses.' She looked at the high walls surrounding the courtyard. 'Tell me, was this once the seraglio?'

'Quite right, and the rooms up there, my mother's and yours, were the women's quarters,' Ahmet told her.

'Ugh, it gives me claustrophobia!' Selma shivered. 'Fancy being condemned to see nothing but that gruesome hillside all your life.' She rose from the table. 'Come along, Ven, and get changed, so we can go where there's some life.'

Venice put on a plain green linen dress, and her straw hat, which she hoped would satisfy Kem. Aziza appeared as they were about to leave and told Selma in halting English that her mistress wished to see her before she went. 'The commissions,' she explained, and Selma looked puzzled.

'I expect she means Zubeyde Hanim wants you to do some shopping for her,' Venice suggested, and the girl nodded her head vigorously.

'*Evet, evet.*'

'Oh, bother,' Selma exclaimed ungraciously. 'I hope she doesn't keep me long. You'd better go and tell the men I've been delayed.'

She followed Aziza humming a pop song as if she had not a care in the world. As Venice descended the stairs she thought that Kem's solicitude was wasted upon Selma. Until either her father's body or wreckage from the boat was found, she would refuse to believe that he had come to grief.

Returning to the arcade, she found only Ahmet was present. He had donned a light jacket over his shirt, since evidently a visit to the town was considered a formal occasion. She was struck afresh by his good looks and wondered vaguely what he looked like in uniform. His bold eyes assessed her appearance as she explained

Selma's delay and she found herself blushing, which annoyed her. There was a sensuousness in his regard which vaguely disturbed her.

'You must not let Kem bore you with discourses about the new republic,' he remarked casually. 'He does not realise foreigners are not interested in our innovations. Personally I regret the old days.'

'You can't be serious?'

'Oh, but I am. I would have been someone important in a less egalitarian society, a pasha or a vizier, with my own harem. Women were kept in their place in those days—no vote, no profession except the oldest one, and subservient to their master's pleasure.'

Venice moved uncomfortably, feeling he was somehow trying to diminish her.

'You can't expect me to sympathise with such a reactionary attitude,' she objected.

A sensual expression crept into the dark expressive eyes.

'Are women really happier for being independent?' he enquired. 'As my concubine you would have been pampered . . . and loved.'

'Oh, really!' she exclaimed. This descent to the personal increased her discomfort. Ahmet seemed to be assessing her as an occupant of the harem he regretted and to her horror she experienced a faint inner excitement in response to his amorousness. The last thing she desired was to become involved emotionally with either of the Osmans, and she uneasily suspected that Ahmet knew how he was affecting her and would attempt to take advantage of it. To change the subject, she said quickly:

'You aren't much like your brother.'

'Totally dissimilar,' he agreed. 'But as you know we have different mothers. Kem is a fanatic, while I am what I believe you call a playboy. I am not really a very

good soldier, but I am not interested in modern war-
fare. Now in the old days, when the Ottoman Army was
a great fighting force, it would have been very different.
We nearly conquered Europe.'

Venice looked at him curiously. She could easily
picture him turbaned and mounted on a great horse,
scimitar in hand, charging into the enemy. But he
was an educated man and the primitive forces which
she sensed in him should have been ironed out of him.
Selma had warned her the savage Ottoman still lay not
far from the surface in her cousins, and this seemed to
be true of Ahmet. A handsome, magnetic brute, she
thought disparagingly, while she strove to subdue the
sexual excitement he aroused in her.

Then to her relief Kemal came out to join them.

'The launch is ready,' he said, and catching her
questioning look, 'yes, we are going by sea.'

'Just in time, dear brother,' Ahmet drawled. 'I was
about to attempt to seduce our charming guest.'

A faint distaste showed on the older man's face.

'I do not like your choice of words,' he said curtly,
'though of course you jest.'

Venice was not so sure about that, and the meaning
look Ahmet gave her did nothing to reassure her. She
was thankful when Selma came running out to them.

'So sorry to keep you waiting, but your mother,' she
glared at Ahmet as if it was his fault, 'wanted so many
things. Does she never go out herself?'

'Rarely,' Ahmet admitted. 'But you wish to go to the
shops, do you not? So we will manage her commissions.
This way, dear cousin.' He put his hand under her
elbow and guided her through the doorway they had
entered by on the previous day. Venice noticed his
action and decided he had been merely amusing himself with her while he waited for the more attractive
girl.

They walked the short distance to the waterfront and after the quiet of the courtyard they seemed to be stepping into a maelstrom of noise. Buses and cars raced along the road, hooting as they went. Radios and transistors blared from the cafés and kiosks, children shouted. Occasionally a ship on the water added to the cacophony with a blast from its siren to warn smaller craft to give it passage.

Selma was excited by the noise and bustle; she seized Ahmet's hand and ran ahead down the sloping path. Kem, following more sedately with Venice, smiled indulgently:

'She is very young, our cousin.'

'Actually she is older than I,' Venice told him.

The keen grey eyes swept over her consideringly.

'In years perhaps,' he said, 'but unlike her you have not been cherished all your life, yes?'

She was astonished by his discernment. 'I lost my parents when I was very young,' she told him. 'The aunt who brought me up didn't believe in spoiling children.'

'Spoiling?' The word in that context seemed to baffle him.

'Well, making a fuss of them,' she explained, and saw sympathetic comprehension in his eyes.

'But that will have made you more self-reliant and perhaps a finer woman. Hardship develops character.'

'No doubt.' She was not sure she appreciated his remarks, they made her sound worthy but unattractive. 'But I could have done with a bit of what you call cherishing.'

'That you will have when you marry.'

Venice laughed. She could not see Bill in the role of cherisher; it was more likely she would find herself looking after him.

They had reached the waterfront where the launch

was moored to a wooden pier. The boy Ismael was seated in the bow and he sprang up as they approached. It was a motor boat with an awning spread over the passenger seats. Creeping up the Bosphorus in midstream was a large cruise ship flying the Greek flag.

Kemal pointed it out to them.

'That is what we want for Turkiye. One or two of those monsters would rake in the tourists' liras, but we have as yet nothing so large.'

Selma said idly: 'Pa's investing in one, isn't he? That should help.'

Venice threw Kem a startled glance. So if anything had happened to Lucas Hadleigh it would hit him hard. The Professor was a very wealthy man and most of his assets were invested abroad, which was partly why he had decided to leave England. His scientific career had been a matter of choice, not necessity; he liked to use his brain. But Selma would presumably inherit a considerable fortune, which would make her doubly attractive to both brothers.

'Your father has been very generous,' Kem told Selma, 'but he is of course entitled to a share of the profits.'

A shadow crossed his face and Venice knew he was thinking, 'If he ever returns.'

He jumped into the launch and Ahmet followed him, turning to help Selma over the thwart with unnecessary elaboration. While he was settling her in her seat, Venice climbed nimbly aboard, refusing Ismael's proffered hand. Kemal had gone to the controls, and after glancing round to be sure they were all embarked, he started the engine. The boat slid away from its mooring and headed for Istanbul.

Venice became absorbed in the scenery. On the Anatolian side, distant mountains could be seen over the low hills rising from the sea. The tall keep of the

Rumeli Hisar rose sheer from the water, while on the opposite shore the battlements of the smaller Anadolu Hisar faced it. There were sandy coves on both shores, and she asked Ahmet eagerly:

'Can one bathe here?'

'Yes, of course,' he indicated the heads of several swimmers. 'But you must be careful not to go far out. There are dangerous currents, strong fresher water from the Black Sea and a saltier one from the Sea of Marmara. They change direction several times a day.'

'Interesting,' Selma said in a bored tone. 'But I can only swim a few strokes.'

'You must look ravishing in a bikini,' Ahmet asserted, looking at her languishingly.

She laughed coquettishly. 'Venice will tell you.'

'Selma always looks ravishing,' Venice returned coolly, Ahmet, she decided, was a flirt.

Every sort of craft was sailing on the blue waters, from small fishing vessels to stately liners. As they neared the port, Venice recognised the long white façade of the Dolmabahce Palace that they had passed on their way in. Was it only yesterday? She felt as if she had been there about a month.

The harbour below the Galata Bridge was crowded with shipping. Another big cruise vessel flying a French flag was being manoevred into its berth by a bustling little Turkish tug, with a Turkish pennant, the crescent and star on a scarlet ground. Ferryboats to Anatolia and the Islands passed and repassed.

Kem steered his craft to a berth on the right-hand bank which appeared to be reserved for him, for the name Osman was stuck up on a board. He killed the engine and Ismael sprang ashore, painter in hand, to secure it to its mooring bollard. A stout gendarme stared at them stonily but made no move. Evidently Kem was well known.

Venice withdrew her gaze from the skyline pierced with the domes and minarets of mosques, and followed Selma on to the quay. It was a steep step up and Ahmet lifted his cousin bodily on to it. He turned back to perform the same service for Venice, but Kemal, already ashore, anticipated him, extending a slim brown hand to assist her. She jumped up lightly, aware that at his touch an electric current had set her nerves quivering. His hold had been so sure and firm, with its aid she could have leaped something much higher than the distance on to the quay.

'Thank you,' she murmured, aware that he did not immediately release his clasp, under the pretext of steadying her.

'Do not go too near the edge,' he warned her, and she had the odd sensation that he too was affected. Hastily she withdrew her fingers, wondering if there was something in the atmosphere of the place that was making her so susceptible. One guide book she had read described the city as having the beauty and fascination of an incredibly old and promiscuous woman who had never washed away her sins. She had thought it overdrawn then, but now she perceived its aptness. That country was very ancient, and Greek, Roman, the Crusaders and the Ottomans had all left their imprint upon it, and contributed to its voluptuous charm. None of its conquerors had been famed for austerity. She stood with Selma looking about her trying to recover her usual cool composure, while the brothers consulted together. Ismael was to stay with the launch and had brought his lunch with him. Venice looked everywhere except at Kemal's lithe trim figure, but irresistibly her eyes kept being drawn towards him. Ridiculous, she scolded herself, you're not a soppy teenager to be thrilled because a personable man has touched your hand. Think about Bill. But Bill did not fit into that environment at all.

Kemal turned towards them. 'I will meet you here at six o'clock,' he told them. Ahmet will show you round. You will find there is plenty to see.'

'Can't you come with us?' Selma asked, making play with her eyelashes. 'Surely you can't be busy when you're on leave?'

He gave her a long wondering look.

'I am afraid it is impossible,' he said curtly. 'Enjoy yourselves.'

Unheeding a further protest from Selma, he left them abruptly, moving away with a long supple stride, and was soon lost in the crowd.

'My brother is what you call ...' Ahmet hesitated, feeling for a word, 'a bit of a boor,' he brought out triumphantly. 'He shows so plainly that his business is more attractive than your company. But we will not mourn for him. Let us cross the bridge.'

'Walk?' Selma asked disgustedly, hanging back.

'Yes, it is not far, and we must show Venice our bridge.'

They moved away from the waterfront.

CHAPTER FOUR

AHMET conducted the two girls away from the water-front through some rather squalid back streets to re-emerge in the space before the Galata Bridge in the heart of the city. Avoiding the broad road across it with its lines of seething traffic, he led them down to a path that ran beside it. Here under the bridge were all kinds of little shops, mostly selling fish and fruit, and even a restaurant. Above them roared the cars and buses, but here the traffic consisted of a few tradesmen's vans and trolleys. They were but a few feet above the water, divided from it by a stranded wire railing, except for a couple of wharves, landing stages for ferries, composed of floating docks.

'Ugh!' Selma wrinkled her nose. 'It smells!'

'Do you not wish to imbibe the atmosphere of the town?' Ahmet asked with seeming gravity, but mischief in his eyes. 'Is it not the tourist's aim to savour the feel of a place?'

'I'm not a tourist, I'm a native,' Selma reminded him. 'But perhaps Ven is enjoying the aroma?' She glanced slyly at her friend.

'It's quaint,' Venice said non-committally. 'But is there no way through for shipping?'

He explained that a span of the bridge was opened very early in the morning to allow vessels to pass. In places the path seemed damp and spongy under her feet and she wondered if it had any solid foundation. Finally it became concrete sloping upwards, and they climbed some steps on to the main road. Here it split into thoroughfares going in all directions, presided over by the minarets of the Yemi Cami or New Mosque. The waters of the Golden Horn reflected the blue of the sky, giving no indication of the pollution that sullied it from the many factories along its banks. Venice could have gone on forever savouring the sights, smells and sounds of this bustling city, but Selma refused to walk any further, so Ahmet stopped a taxi and they were driven to the Grand Bazaar. Here Selma was in her element, wandering among the brilliantly lit arcades mostly displaying tourist goods, and Venice had to remind her of their hostess's commissions. These she executed perfunctorily, handing her parcels to Ahmet to carry, and then announced that she was ready for lunch. This entailed another taxi ride, this time over the other newer bridge into the more modern part of the town, the Beyoglu district, where once the foreign settlements had been. Ahmet took them to a westernised restaurant where the food was European and they could eat out of doors on a terrace roofed with a trellised vine which gave it a pleasant shade, and from which they had a fine view over the three waters, the Marmara, the Bosphorus and the Golden Horn, for it was at Istanbul that they met.

When they had eaten neither Ahmet nor Selma seemed inclined to move, and Venice, who was longing to go back and explore the historic buildings in the old town, had to control her impatience. To her tentative hints, Selma returned that one mosque was much like another and having seen one you had seen all and there was plenty of time. Venice, who had seen none as yet, sighed and continued to contemplate the view. It was particularly trying for her because the other two were indulging in a low-voiced flirtation that excluded her. Ahmet, she decided viciously, was fickle, and she felt ashamed of her former reactions to him. No doubt he found Selma more responsive, which was as it should be, and she wished Bill were with her. Surely his insularity would be overcome by the splendid panorama spread out before her.

At last Selma rose and requested her to accompany her to the powder room. There she spent such an inordinate time making up her face that Venice left her to it and returned to the terrace. She leaned on the balustrade absorbing the view, and Ahmet came to join her.

'You must forgive my neglect,' he said with one of his soft glances at her pure profile beside him. 'But it is necessary I must do my best to cheer the little one, is it not? We cannot let her grieve over her father's fate.'

'I quite understand,' Venice returned acidly, wondering why he thought it was necessary to excuse his attentions to Selma, who did not seem to be grieving in the least. 'Selma is so lovely,' she went on. 'I'm used to retiring into the shade when she's around.'

To her astonishment he announced: 'She is pretty, yes, but I have known many girls who look as she does. Now you, you intrigue me, with your Nordic fairness. You look so remote and cool, but I am sure there is fire under the ice. Any man would find you a challenge.'

'I don't know what you mean by that,' she retorted, uncomfortably aware that he was almost touching her as they leant over the balustrade. 'I'm a very ordinary English girl and I'm not feeling neglected, so you needn't try to flatter me, though I'm not sure your remarks were flattering.'

'It is because you are English I find you so different,' he said earnestly. 'Selma is a daughter of the East, I find her obvious. Now you, you have the waxen delicacy of a magnolia ...'

'Oh, please stop,' she laughed, reflecting that Ahmet had probably had more success with Northern tourist girls than was good for him. 'Such similes don't cut any ice with me, I doubt their sincerity.' She sighed. 'Do you think we'll have time to visit Saint Sophia? Unlike Selma, I've never seen a mosque and I'm dying to visit some of the famous sights.'

Ahmet looked a little piqued.

'So you would find that old museum more amusing than myself?'

'I don't think amusing is quite the right word,' she countered.

'Perhaps my English is at fault?'

'It is almost too perfect.'

'We were taught to speak it correctly at school,' he told her stiffly. He leaned closer to look into her face. 'But there is one word that needs no translation in any language.' His dark eyes were eloquent.

'You're wasting your time,' she said crisply, though her heart quickened its beat as she met the ardour in his eyes. 'I have a boy-friend back in England.'

'A boy-friend? Ah, you mean a lover. He must be slow, that one, not to have made a woman of you.'

'Oh, really!' Venice flushed indignantly. 'I'm not promiscuous.'

He was quick to rectify his mistake. 'What I meant was you do not have the bloom of a woman who is desired and desires,' he explained airily. 'Contrary to what you may imagine, we are not promiscuous either. We respect the flower that is unplucked. I would never wed another man's cast-off. But you English are ... what you say ... cold fish.'

Somewhat to her relief, Venice saw Selma approaching.

'Not quarrelling, you two?' she asked suspiciously, glancing from Venice's slightly flushed face to Ahmet's mocking one.

'Of course not,' Venice said quickly. 'Why should we quarrel?'

'Oh, I don't know,' Selma shrugged her shoulders. 'You look a bit prickly, Ven, and I thought Ahmet might be getting fresh.' She shot him a provocative glance from under her lashes.

'Fresh?' he did not understand her, but Venice's conscious look betrayed her.

'We were behaving with perfect propriety,' she said hastily.

'I should hope so, in a public place,' Selma opined sedately. 'But there was no one to overhear what he said.'

'I only paid her a few compliments which she seemed to resent,' Ahmet told her sulkily. 'I do not understand the women of the West.'

'You will,' Selma assured him solemnly. She whispered aside to Venice, as he moved away, 'No trespassing!'

Venice felt an unusual flash of resentment. Selma took it for granted that every unattached male was her preserve. Then she recalled what he had said about her friend and reflected that Selma was wasting her time, unless his comments had been insincere, which they probably were. He surprised her by turning back to say:

'Venice wishes to be taken to Aya Sofya.'

'What energy!' Selma sighed. 'I doubt my feet will support me to go sightseeing. My shoes are killing me.'

Selma had small and pretty feet and she meant to draw Ahmet's attention to them. He obligingly looked down at her high-heeled white sandals, which looked far too flimsy for serious use.

'Then we will go to the Sultan Ahmet Mosque which you call the Blue Mosque and then you will have to take them off.'

Venice said eagerly, 'Is it so sacred?'

'That is not the reason. The foreheads of the faithful

contact the carpets when they perform their devotions and therefore they must be kept clean.'

'Oh!' Venice exclaimed, disappointed by this prosaic explanation. 'I thought it had to do with putting the shoes off one's feet because one was standing upon holy ground.'

'There may have been something like that at one time, but now we are practical,' he returned. 'Some mosques provide over-shoes, but not Sultan Ahmet's, but you can keep them on in Aya Sofya, that is a museum now.'

In the end they went to both, since they are not far apart. Venice was duly impressed by the soaring domes and massive pillars, and the Blue Mosque enchanted her with its blue tiling that gave it its name. She discreetly kept her eyes away from the few kneeling figures who were saying their prayers. Ahmet had explained that the Turks were much more tolerant than their Arab neighbours, who often refused to allow infidels into their sacred buildings.

There were long racks outside in the courtyard to accommodate the visitors' shoes, and Selma made a great fuss about removing her sandals, making Ahmet undo and re-fasten the straps, kneeling beside her while she support herself with a hand upon his shoulder, while she smiled triumphantly at Venice over his bowed dark head. Venice was wearing ballerina slip-ons which were no trouble, and she was diverted by Selma's tactics, wondering what impression they made upon Ahmet. Not very great, she decided, for when he stood up he too flashed her a glance full of cynical amusement.

They admired the gardens of the hippodrome with its Egyptian obelisks. The whole space, including the ground upon which the Blue Mosque was built, had once been a racecourse.

Ahmet said it was a pity the tulips were over—the tulip was originally brought to Britain from Turkey—and they had not time to visit the Topkapi palace and museum but must leave it for another day, a statement Selma heartily endorsed. Even Venice was beginning to feel tired.

The shadows were beginning to lengthen when they arrived back at the quayside and found Kemal there before them. He came to meet them with an air of suppressed excitement so that Venice was sure he had news for them. Ahmet said before he could speak:

'You have information, my brother?'

'Yes.' He looked at Selma. 'I think we have found your father.'

'Found him?' she asked blankly. 'Where? Why hasn't he come to meet me?'

'Because he is ill, little one,' Kem said gently. 'Though I am sure he will soon recover. He is only suffering from exposure and exhaustion.'

Selma had been so sure he would appear hale and hearty that this information frightened her. Clasping her hands, she asked hollowly, while she stared at Kem:

'You mean he is dying?'

'Far from it,' he replied reassuringly. 'It would take more than a few days at sea to kill the Professor Bey.'

Selma clutched his arm. 'I must go to him.'

Venice felt a surge of relief, but she was sure Kemal was keeping something back. She was ashamed that she had ever doubted Selma's affection for her father; now she realised he had been in danger, she was overwhelmed, and her expression was that of the Tragic Muse.

Kem put a comforting arm about her and led her towards the boat.

'Come, we must get you home.'

'But I must go to Pa,' she cried distractedly. 'Where

is he? In hospital? You will take me to him?'

'You shall go as soon as it is possible,' he soothed her. 'But you cannot go without preparation.' He helped her down into the boat. 'You see, he is in a sanatorium at Yalta. He was picked up by a Russian ship when he was drifting with a broken engine and a broken rudder across the Black Sea.'

'Yalta?' Selma asked sharply. 'Where's that?'

By this time, Venice and Ahmet had climbed down into the boat, but Selma still clung to Kem and he could not start the engine. Ismael had risen to greet them and stood with the mooring rope in his hand waiting.

'All right, cast off,' Kem said, disentangling himself from Selma. He pushed her down beside Venice. 'Excuse me.' He went to manipulate the controls.

'Yalta is in the Crimea,' Venice told Selma, wondering how much of Kem's story was true. Had Lucas Hadleigh really been picked up, or had he been deliberately abducted? Questioningly she sought Kem's eyes over Selma's head and he smiled at her reassuringly.

'He *was* shipwrecked,' he said, and turned his attention to guiding his craft through the variegated mass of shipping gathered about the approach to the Galata Bridge.

'I have heard Yalta is a beautiful place,' Ahmet told them, 'and I am sure he will be given first-class attention there.'

'But how do I get there?' Selma wailed.

'I will get you there,' Kem promised.

'What, now? Can this boat cross the Black Sea?'

'No, and you cannot go yet. It is impossible to enter Soviet territory without making arrangements.'

'Meanwhile he may die!' Selma as usual was wringing all the drama she could from the situation.

'He is not going to die.' Kem sounded a little impatient. 'From the report I received he is recovering fast. As I said, I will take you to him, but first we have to have visas and obtain a place on a plane or a ship.'

'But that'll take ages,' Selma objected. She began to cry, great tears welling up into her beautiful eyes. She had managed to make weeping a fine art, and was fortunate that neither her eyes nor her nose reddened. The tears simply dripped down her cheeks, if anything enhancing her looks. That they affected the two young men was apparent. Kem coughed and became absorbed in his steering. Ahmet produced a clean white handkerchief, while Ismael stared at her in fascination.

'Please do not cry,' Ahmet besought her. 'I am sure everything will be all right.'

Selma sniffed, while Venice took the handkerchief and mopped her face.

'Cheer up, old girl,' she said brightly. 'Your father has been found and is in good hands. It might have been so much worse.'

'Russian hands,' Selma moaned, refusing to be comforted.

'Their hospital service is excellent, I believe,' Ahmet told her.

Venice whispered in Selma's ear: 'Your make-up is running.'

This had much more effect than the men's attempts at consolation. Selma ceased to weep and fumbled in her bag for a mirror. Venice met Ahmet's eyes and saw derision in them. He believed Selma was putting on an act. Quick to defend her friend, she said:

'She really does care about her father.'

'Of course I do,' Selma cried angrily. 'Just because I put on a brave face and didn't betray how anxious I was, you think I'm callous!' She glared at Ahmet.

'Oh, no, no!' He waved his hands to disclaim such an

accusation. 'I think you are wonderful.'

Selma looked doubtful, as if she felt this description could be taken in more ways than one. She drew away from Venice and declared vehemently:

'I'm not insensitive like Ven, nothing can disturb her cool, but I feel things tremendously.'

Venice was stung by the injustice of this remark, knowing that she had been far more anxious than Selma had been, but then Kem had not told Selma what he had feared. She was still not sure that he had disclosed everything. Lucas Hadleigh was safe and apparently Selma could obtain permission to visit him, Kem would not have promised that if there were any obstacle, but would they both be allowed to leave?

The setting sun drew pencils of gold over the blue water, but in the north-east storm clouds were gathering, blowing in from the Kara Deniz, the Black Sea. To Venice's excited fancy they seemed symbolical. What, she wondered, awaited her friend in that guarded land?

Zubeyde Hanim was delighted when she was told that the Professor had been found. The whole family not only respected him but were fond of him, regarding him as one of themselves through his marriage to Yasmin. In spite of her impatience, Selma could not go at once. As well as a visa she would have to wait for a berth or a seat in a plane and as it was the holiday season most of them were fully booked. Kem assured her over and over again that he was doing his best to expedite matters, and presented her with a set of forms to fill in. To her astonishment he passed one to Venice too.

'But is it necessary for me to go too?' she asked, fearing it would be expensive.

They had finished dinner and were drinking the thick sweet Turkish coffee in the sitting room, for it was a chilly and overcast evening. It was the evening after the day they had spent in Istanbul and Kem had spent most of the morning and afternoon making contacts on Selma's behalf, while Ahmet did his best to console her.

Selma said quickly: 'I'll be all right with Kem. Ven can stay here and amuse Ahmet.'

'Of course she must go with you,' Zubeyde told her sternly. 'You cannot travel with a young man alone. That is why she came here, did she not? To be your chaperone.'

She did not mean it unkindly, but Venice felt depressed at being relegated to the position of a permanent gooseberry. Still, she must do something to repay the Hadleighs' generosity, and if her presence was considered a protection for the wayward Selma she ought not to complain.

Noticing Selma's rebellious expression, Ahmet drawled:

'Though women are now emancipated, dear cousin, you should still consider your good name. You would lessen your desirability as a wife if it were thought you had had affairs with men.'

'But I don't want to have an affair with anyone,' Selma cried indignantly. 'I'm only going to see my father.'

'If you travel alone with a young man, even one as proper as Kem, nobody would believe you had not.'

'I suppose you're referring to your neighbours,' Selma said loftily. 'They're nothing to do with me.'

Zubeyde bristled. 'They may be one day,' she declared significantly, 'and we have our good name to preserve. Kemal is a public man, you know.'

'Oh, very well,' Selma surrendered ungraciously. Then with a swift change of mood she smiled at Venice. 'Sorry, Ven, I didn't mean I didn't want you. Of course

I'll be glad of your company, only it seems a bit absurd to take a whole party to visit a man in hospital.'

'It will be more than that,' Kemal warned her. He had held aloof from the discussion, watching them with a slightly sardonic smile. 'We may have to stay for a few days until the Professor Bey is pronounced fit to travel. We shall want to bring him back with us.'

Venice looked at him a little reproachfully. So there was no doubt that the Professor would be allowed to leave, but although he had admitted to her the possibility that he might be detained, he had not bothered to relieve her anxiety when he discovered all was well. Then she reflected that he had not had an opportunity to speak to her alone since contacting the Soviet authorities, and he had not told anybody else of his fears.

Ahmet said negligently: 'I might as well come along too to complete the expedition.' He looked from Selma to Venice as if expecting an invitation.

'Ah, no, my son,' Zubeyde protested. 'That would not do at all. Then there would be two pairs which would cause the gossip. You must stay here and look after me.'

Ahmet did not look as though he appreciated that prospect, but he made no protest. Zubeyde might appear to be soft and indolent, but her word was law in that household. Two pairs seemed a perfectly normal arrangement to Venice's Western mind; she could only suppose that Zubeyde feared Ahmet might become too interested in the wrong girl, so preferred to keep him under her eye, though that idea was ludicrous. True, Ahmet had made some overtures towards her, but that might have been an attempt to discover if she were available. She could never seriously rival the glamorous Selma, who had the additional advantage of being well gilded. She wondered if Selma had any preference between the two brothers or was merely amusing herself by playing one off against the other. She was in her element that evening, seated on a divan between the two men, her lovely face aglow with coquetry. Both were endeavouring to assist her to fill in the forms, and she was doing her best to drag out the process.

Venice sat a little apart, with her papers upon her knee, and Zubeyde behind the coffee pot was watching the trio on the divan intently, perhaps asking herself the same question that Venice had formulated. She was oblivious apparently of the explosiveness of the situation, for if two dogs want the same bone neither would surrender without a fight. If Zubeyde favoured her son's suit, surely she would be wiser to allow him to accompany Selma to the Crimea, but possibly she did not and that was the reason for her veto.

Suddenly Kemal stood up, and thrust the papers and Selma's passport into his briefcase.

'That is that one done. Now, Venice,' he moved towards her, 'come into my work room. We will complete yours more quickly without interruptions.'

Surprised, Venice looked up at him, while Selma protested:

'Why the ceremony? Can't she do it here, like I did?'

'And look what a time it has taken,' he returned impatiently. 'I have some telephoning to do when we have finished, and also I promised to lend Venice a book. She can choose one when she is in there.'

'Presumably one about our lost leader,' Ahmet suggested insolently. 'I suppose she expressed polite interest in your enthusiasms and you are about to take her up on it. Poor girl, she will find the subject tedious.'

'Oh, no, I shan't,' Venice declared, getting to her feet. She was annoyed by Ahmet's tone and wanted to reassure Kemal. She went swiftly out of the room with

76

heightened colour, aware that she had left speculation behind her.

Kemal's work room, as he called it, was in front of the house, and through the uncurtained windows the Bosphorus was visible, the lights on the further shore shining like fireflies against the velvet dark. There was less traffic on the road below them than in the daytime, and a golden haze obscured the buildings along the waterfront. Passing ships moved like glittering galaxies. Venice leaned against the window frame looking out. Throbbing music from stringed instruments reached her from some place of entertainment beneath them, sensuous and exciting, indubitably a love song.

'How pretty it looks,' she said dreamily. 'I much prefer this side to the back of the house. What a pity more rooms don't have this view.'

'The people who built it preferred seclusion,' Kemal told her. 'It is only of late years that we have opened our windows to the world.'

She turned round and saw that he was watching her enigmatically and her heart missed a beat. The intensity of his keen gaze disturbed her, and she became very conscious that they were alone. She would have been wiser to insist upon remaining with the others.

'You mean since the republic was inaugurated?' she said vaguely, her mind more occupied by the man than his words.

'Exactly. Will you sit down?'

He indicated a round leather chair before his desk. The furnishing of the room was functional—a big desk, his swivel chair, behind it a couple of leather chairs in one of which she seated herself as instructed, a bookcase, filing cabinet and other office equipment. Conspicuous on the wall behind the desk was a framed photograph surrounded by a laurel wreath, and hung above it the Turkish flag. Venice did not need to ask whom it commemorated. Kemal sat down behind his desk and pushed the forms over to her, showing her where to sign her name, and asked her a few curt questions. When they had finished, she looked up at the pictured face behind him, and said:

'I'm surprised you didn't choose the Army for your career. He was a great soldier, wasn't he?'

'A military genius,' Kemal replied. 'Like Napoleon, but unlike him, he had no wish for territorial gains, he only wanted to free his country from the foreign yoke. In his day I should certainly have been in the Army, but now I feel I can serve Turkey better in other ways. Ataturk created a nation, but now we have to make it prosper. We have a great asset in tourism, we have much to show to visitors, not only Istanbul but Erzerum, Izmir, even the ruins of Troy. Hence my interest in the business, but much more than that, I have been elected to the National Assembly, and once I am fully recovered, I shall spend most of my time in Ankara.' He moved out from behind his desk and began to pace the small room, his lithe spare frame vibrant with energy, his eyes shining fixed upon some distant vision. 'There is so much to be done. Education—there are still far too many illiterate children, but in Anatolia the parents want to keep them to work on the farms and the distances are so great. Those difficulties must be overcome.' Venice was sure that he had forgotten to whom he was speaking. 'We have mineral resources that need developing, farm land that needs fertilizing, but we are a poor nation. We must find capital, investors . . .' He continued with his hopes and plans, sometimes relapsing into his own language. Venice suspected that ambition went hand in hand with his patriotism; the National Assembly was only a stepping stone to higher office. Something of his white-hot ardour spread to her, creating an inner excitement.

Like his famous predecessor he had the magnetism that goes with a dynamic personality, the gift of being able to inspire others to follow his leadership. Suddenly he stopped and looked at her apologetically.

'Forgive me, Venice Hanim, I become carried away by my dreams. Unfortunately, though the spirit may be willing it wears out the flesh. I have been ordered to rest, but I cannot wait to be in the saddle again.'

'You mustn't be in too great a hurry,' she said prosaically, 'or you'll only be ill again.'

He made a contemptuous gesture. 'I know better than the doctors when I am fit to return. My weakness was due to a fever, but it has left me now. When we have brought the Professor Bey back from Yalta, I shall be returning to the capital. I have a house there.'

'And you will perhaps marry?' Venice asked, thinking of Selma. She doubted if that vivacious lady would think much of living in Ankara, which she had heard was situated on an isolated plateau with a climate of extremes.

'Possibly,' he said without enthusiasm. 'If I can find the right woman. Ataturk preached that a wife should stand side by side with her husband, helping with his work.' He smiled with sudden elusive charm. 'But I fear I shall not make a good husband.'

'No worse than most,' she declared, 'but I think your ... your leader was wrong. A clever ambitious man needs a wife for relaxation, a home bird, without too many brains.'

She was still thinking of Selma. She had been trained as a teacher, so she might be able to assist Kemal with his educational projects, but she did not believe Selma meant to practise her profession when she married.

She became aware that the grey eyes were regarding her quizzically.

'Then you would not qualify, would you, for I think you possess much intelligence.'

She flushed as she said quickly: 'I was speaking impersonally.'

'A wife is hardly an impersonal subject, but women are always obsessed by the romantic image,' he observed, smiling derisively. 'Believe me, romance plays a very small part in my life.'

She remembered that this man was a Turk and blurted out:

'But aren't they necessary?'

His face became a cold mask. 'We were discussing matrimony,' he said stiffly.

Venice could have kicked herself for her unfortunate remark; used to plain and even bawdy talk among her college friends, she had forgotten where she was and to whom she was speaking.

'Forgive me, I'm trespassing,' she said gently.

'You are,' he retorted. He moved swiftly to the bookcase and began to select several volumes. 'If you are really interested, I have several biographies of Ataturk.'

'I'd love to read them,' she told him, though she eyed the volumes a little apprehensively. They looked tough.

He thrust them into her arms. 'Then if you will excuse me, as I said I have some telephoning to do.'

Dismissed and with unnecessary abruptness, she thought as she left the room. Kemal was regretting that he had exposed so much of his mind to her, and yet she felt intuitively that there was something between them that neither wanted to acknowledge, almost an affinity. But even as the thought took form, she scolded herself for being ridiculous. Between her and the rising politician there could be nothing except a polite interest on her part and a courteous tolerance on his.

She slipped up to her room with the books, unwilling to allow Ahmet an opportunity to jibe at her ... and him. She then returned to the sitting room to find Zubeyde had retired and Ahmet and Selma were still on the divan in close conversation, with a box of candy on the table before them. She was surprised that their hostess had left them alone after her remarks about a chaperone, but perhaps she did not consider surveillance was necessary inside the house where neighbours could not pry. Looking at the two dark heads so close together she thought her speculations about Kemal and Selma had been beside the point. If any couple were going to fall in love it would be these two. She was surprised at the relief she felt. She was about to withdraw when Ahmet sensed her presence and looked up.

'Come and join us,' he said, patting the divan on his other side. 'You have been a long time.'

'Oh, I haven't been all this time with Kem,' she told him, instinctively wanting to conceal what had transpired between her and the other man. 'I went up to my room to tidy myself.'

Ahmet grinned mischievously. 'Did Kem forget himself?'

'Of course not.' She hoped she had not blushed. The mere suggestion that that dedicated person could be sufficiently interested in her humble self to make a pass at her was utterly incongruous. 'We had business to transact,' she reminded him frigidly. Instead of accepting Ahmet's invitation she walked back to her chair.

A malicious gleam came into his dark eyes.

'You do not imagine my brother is an ascetic?'

Ahmet had no inhibitions about plain speaking, she thought, as she returned coldly, 'I'm not interested in Kem's love life.' But she remembered how his face had changed when she asked her indiscreet question. Well, she did not suppose he was a monk.

Selma intervened. 'Ven doesn't like that sort of remark. She's a bit pi and not at all sexy.'

'You are singularly unobservant, Selma,' Ahmet told her, his eyes still on Venice. 'Your friend may be asleep, but she is not an iceberg. One day she will surprise you.'

'Now don't go getting ideas,' Selma tapped his arm playfully. 'I should know her better than you do.'

'Dear cousin, no woman can possibly know how her sister behaves when she is alone with a man.'

'But Ven isn't my sister ... Oh, I see, you're speaking generally. You think you're awfully smart about girls, don't you, Ahmet, but you don't know as much as you think you do.' She smiled at him provocatively. 'About English girls, that is.'

'I assure you no respectable Turkish girl would behave like you do,' he returned.

'No? I thought they were emancipated now.'

'They are, theoretically, but they are careful to preserve their integrity.'

Selma's dark brows drew together, and she slapped his face.

'Do you think I don't value mine?' she snapped.

Venice rose to her feet. 'Different countries, different manners,' she observed in a conciliatory tone. 'Don't judge us by our free speech, Ahmet, it's a revolt from hypocrisy. I'm going to bed, Selma. Are you coming?'

Ahmet said penitently, 'Wait until I have made my apologies.' But his insolent eyes held no remorse.

'Selma will accept them, no doubt,' Venice smiled. 'Goodnight, Ahmet.'

He looked at her beseechingly. 'Please stay, Venice, I am afraid to be alone with this wildcat here.'

'You can cope with her,' she returned, shaking her head. 'Goodnight.'

Incorrigible flirt, she thought as she went upstairs, but Selma can handle him without my help. She enjoys that sort of backchat. It seemed empty and trivial to her after the exhilaration of Kemal's outpouring. It did not occur to her that a similar discourse from another man might have bored her. It was the man himself, his dynamic personality that had thrilled her, and that became even more apparent as settled in bed with her table lamp on she started to read the books he had lent to her. Selma came up much later but did not come in to her, fearing censure. Venice did not notice the sounds in the bathroom and eventual quiet; she was absorbed in her reading. She was horrified and shocked by the accounts of the savagery of the fighting between Greek and Turk, the destruction of non-combatants, but the grim determination of the Turkish leader against overwhelming odds evoked her admiration. Unconsciously she began to identify him with the Kemal Osman she knew. The man's magnetism and fascination reached her from the printed pages. Like Kem he had been fair, grey-eyed and of unheroic stature. The author of one book described him as a grey wolf, and in some ways the simile was apt. Venice had always admired men of action, and this one, with everything against him, had fired a decadent and divided people with loyalty and patriotism. Ruthless he had been, but he had been able to command devotion. She read with awe the account of the Anatolian women who, because transport was so short, carried ammunition and supplies on their backs right up to the front line, unsung heroines. Then the aftermath, the dictator's uncompromising stripping away of convention, tradition, and religious prejudice to create the modern state he had envisaged. She knew now why the Turks called him 'our saviour.'

Kem was inspired by the same fiery patriotism, devoting himself to carrying out his hero's aims. He might one day also become a great man. This coupling of his identity with that of his great predecessor was more dangerous than Venice knew. It meant the young Turk was gaining a hold upon her imagination than would be far stronger than anything physical. As regards romance, Ataturk had married, but the marriage had collapsed after a short while. She remembered that Kem had said he would not make a good husband, and he must have been thinking of his hero's matrimonial failure. Ahmet had said he was not as ascetic, but woman-like she thought none the worse of him for that. It was no compliment to a woman when a man shuns her sex and a big one when she wins him against competition. Hard-driven men needed relaxation.

It was nearly dawn when Venice finally closed her books and fell into a troubled sleep. In her dreams Kem and Ataturk were inextricably mixed, and she was pursued by grey wolves with slavering jaws and glittering eyes.

CHAPTER FIVE

THERE were no seats available on a flight to the Crimea at that time of year, the peak of the holiday season, but Kemal obtained accommodation for them on a cruise vessel that had put into Istanbul. The journey would take longer by sea, but it had the advantage of going from door to door. It was a Greek ship, but Kemal had a business connection with the Captain, who informed him that he had a spare cabin for the girls, if he did not mind sharing with a member of the crew himself. 'A little palm oil did the trick,' Kem told the girls.

How soon they could return depended upon the Professor's state of health and how much red tape had to be unwound. It was not even certain the castaway was Lucas Hadleigh, though from the description Kem had no doubt about that. He had had no papers with him, so he would have to be identified officially. Selma's presence was necessary to vouch for her parent.

The liner was a fast modern ship and would take about fourteen hours to cross the Black Sea. They left in the afternoon and expected to arrive the following morning. Selma was jubilant that her optimism about her father had been justified and she spent a hectic evening with the passengers, as there was dancing after dinner. Kemal, having a kindred interest, went into a huddle with the cruise manager and the purser, and Venice went up on deck to watch the stars come out over the quiet sea. She felt reluctant to join the lively crowds in the lounges, dimly aware of some change within herself, a sharpening of her senses to a new appreciation of the beauty of the sea and sky, a sen-

suous dreaminess that she would not admit had anything to do with Kemal Osman. When he came to fetch
her for a drink before she retired, she should have been
warned, for the sight of his spruce well-groomed figure
caused her heart to leap, but she assured herself it was
only because his sudden appearance startled her. She
was past the age of girlish crushes, she told herself, and
he was practically a stranger, an intriguing one no
doubt, but quite ineligible as far as she was concerned.

He escorted her down into one of the lounges, and
found a secluded table by a window. A waiter took his
order for drinks.

Although Islam frowns upon alcohol, he drank it in
moderation, saying it was necessary to do so when
entertaining foreign clients, and from her reading
Venice knew that Ataturk, upon whom he modelled
himself, had no inhibitions about it. Tonight he talked
mainly about the Osmans' shipping interests, and the
big cruise ship that the Government was hoping to
build. It would provide many jobs and it would make a
lot of money.

'We need both,' he said. 'Like everywhere else we
have an unemployment problem.'

But though he talked of impersonal matters his eyes
dwelt upon Venice with warm appreciation. The black
dress she wore showed off the whiteness of her neck
and shoulders which had not had time to tan, and en-
hanced her fairness. A necklace of Irish diamonds,
semi-precious stones, brought out the green in her eyes.
She had a feeling of well-being in his presence; they
seemed to be en rapport, she decided, but there could
never be anything between them except friendship.
After a silence during which they watched the pro-
cession of gaily clad figures passing through the centre
of the lounge, she enquired tentatively:

'Do you believe that men and women can be friends? Platonically, I mean.'

He replied with a hint of violence that surprised her.

'Never, except possibly occasionally when they have first been lovers.'

Disappointed, she turned her head away. 'You mean a man's interest is always sexual?'

'Of course,' he returned brusquely, as if he found the subject distasteful. 'And a woman's too. Without the lure of femininity, men prefer to make comrades of other men.'

'Then, when you talk to me, you're just being polite?' She regretted the words as soon as she had uttered them; she had meant to avoid the personal issue.

His grey eyes became quizzical. 'I thought we were speaking of generalities,' he rebuked her.

'Yes, of course,' she said hurriedly, and changed the subject by remarking: 'I wonder what Selma is doing. It's getting very late.'

'Demoralising the male passengers,' he said with a grin, then added more kindly: 'It is good to see her so happy now her father is safe.'

But Selma had never believed he was anything else.

When a few minutes later Venice said goodnight to Kemal, he told her:

'If ever a woman could be a man's friend it would be you. You are not only sensible but loyal and sincere.'

Words which did not please her, for she realised as she entered her cabin, leaving him on the threshold, that she was kidding herself with talk of friendship. She would like to be so maddeningly alluring that she was irresistible and could bring Kemal to her feet. The qualities he had mentioned, although estimable, suggested a Girl Guide or the schoolmarm she was fated to be. For the first time she was really envious of Selma's looks and charm.

Venice was up on deck early next morning to watch their approach to Yalta. The bulk of the mountains was the first thing that she saw, rising up out of the sea, pearl grey craggy heights above the morning mists. Gradually the mist cleared and details of the scene became clear. Yalta was ringed with precipitous hills, below which were wooded foothills, houses and gardens. There were many large white buildings that had once been the Grand Dukes' summer palaces, and at the waterline were beaches of golden sand. She had only very vague ideas about the Crimea, mostly culled from films showing a somewhat arid landscape, and she was quite unprepared for Yalta's breathtaking beauty.

Going ashore was a complicated business. They had to queue for landing cards and queue again for what seemed ages to disembark. There were several hundred passengers and as each one appeared on the gangway, his or her passport was scrutinised by two men in uniform and compared with their photographs, the details noted, unlike the cursory glance bestowed at most foreign ports. The Russians were thorough. This took time, and when it came to their turn, the officer signed to them to stand aside and they had to wait until all the cruise passengers had gone ashore. Then he escorted them down the gangway and into the Customs shed. There was a cleared space where the ship was docked, and a stout barricade divided it from the road. A sentry marched up and down to preclude possible intruders. A small crowd of natives stood at the barrier, watching the new arrivals as if they were strange animals escaped from the zoo. Behind them were the gardens and villas which Kem warned them they would not be allowed to roam among without being escorted.

In the Customs hall every article in their luggage was examined and the girls had to turn out their handbags. The official and Kemal had a long discussion over their papers; the man's English was too basic to be useful and they relapsed into French, which both spoke well, so that Venice had no clue as to what it was all about. Finally they were ushered into a car to be driven to the hospital.

'What was the hitch?' Selma asked.

The three of them were sitting in the back seat while their guide, or guard, Venice was not sure in which category he came, sat in front with the chaffeur.

'It seemed Venice has to be pigeonholed,' Kemal explained with a glint of amusement in his eyes. 'I am of course your cousin, and your necessary male escort, but Venice had no connection with us, so I said she was my betrothed.'

'That was rather officious of you,' Venice objected, a bright colour suffusing her face.

'It was not meant to be so, but it gave you status. Very suspicious people, these officials.'

Selma giggled. 'Ven is put out because she has a fiancé in England and he might not be amused if he came to hear about it.'

'Is that so?' Kem gave Venice a surprised glance.

'It isn't official,' Venice said quickly, guiltily aware that she had given Bill few thoughts since she had come abroad.

'And he does not mind this separation?'

'Oh no, he's pleased I should have a chance to see another country.'

Kemal regarded her thoughtfully. 'I find that most strange.'

'They're a cold-blooded pair,' Selma said flippantly. 'Both dedicated teachers.'

Kemal's face lighted up with enthusiasm. 'Ah, what

could be more worthy than to stand side by side presenting the benefits of education to young eager minds?' He glanced at Selma. 'But you were trained to be a teacher too?'

'Yes, but I don't intend to stand beside anyone dishing out the three Rs,' Selma said tartly.

Kem seemed about to expostulate, but the car drew up in front of a long white building set among feathery mimosas, long past their flowering.

There was a further wait and a scrutiny of papers before they were admitted to the wards. Professor Hadleigh was in a small room on his own. He greeted them enthusiastically and seemed little the worse for his adventure, and was sitting in a chair wearing a borrowed dressing gown.

'I hope you've arranged to get me out of here,' he told them.

'I'm doing my best,' Kem said, 'but there will be more formalities, I suppose. Why did you have to get yourself picked up by a Soviet boat?'

'I was in a state when I was thankful to be picked up by anything,' the Professor confessed ruefully. 'Oh, I've nothing to complain of, food's excellent, ditto nursing, but I'm bored stiff, nobody to talk to and no English papers.' He looked at the two girls apologetically. 'Poor sort of start to your holidays. How are you managing?'

'Fine,' Selma told him, glancing coquettishly at Kemal. 'Zubeyde Hanim has taken us in and Ahmet makes sure we're kept amused. Kem is usually too busy.'

Lucas Hadleigh laughed. 'Naturally, my dear boy, we know what heavy responsibilities you carry.' He looked fondly at his daughter. 'My little girl has become very bonny, hasn't she? Can't she divert you from your duties?'

'I've tried,' Selma remarked demurely, 'but without

much success.' Again her eyes sought Kemal's.

'If anyone could divert me, it would be you,' Kem said gallantly, returning her gaze.

Venice felt a sharp prick of chagrin. Kemal had not paid Selma any conspicuous attention, but she herself had had several long conversations with him. Were they too serious to be termed diversions? She recalled that Selma was on offer, so to speak, to both brothers, and she was, as Selma had remarked, involved with Bill. Selma's revelation would have killed any dawning interest Kemal might have felt in her, which was as it should be. Why then should she mind if he paid Selma compliments, albeit it was a slightly ambiguous one? No reason at all, except that she doubted his sincerity.

They left after about half an hour and were conducted to the hotel where reservations had been made for them. Their guide discoursed at length upon the amenities of Yalta, which had become a convalescent centre for tired workers and provided a specially good climate for tubercular patients, for whom many sanatoriums had been built. He gave them a list of statistics illustrating Soviet progress, of which Venice took in very little and Selma was plainly not listening.

Selma had promised to visit the Professor again in the afternoon when he was to be allowed to take a walk in the grounds. Venice refused her invitation to join them, thinking father and daughter might like to be alone. Kemal went off to make arrangements for their return and she was left to her own devices. He had warned her not to leave the hotel grounds to explore as she would have liked to do.

'They do not like people wandering about alone,' he told her. 'You might get picked up by the police and have difficulty in explaining yourself.'

'They wouldn't arrest me?'

'No, but you would be escorted back to the hotel.'

She was inclined to test the truth of his apprehensions. The beach, which she could see from the eminence on which the hotel was built, looked inviting though crowded, but she was a foreigner and would not be able to make herself understood if she found herself in difficulties, which might reverberate on to Kemal, who had enough to arrange without being involved in her indiscretions. She had better do what she had been told. She bought a guide book in the foyer, for which the vendor accepted eagerly an English pound when she said she had no roubles. From it she learned that the forests clothing the lower slopes of the mountains were Crimean pines with a bark of a peculiar light grey and needles of an unusually bright green. The cypresses, a decorative feature of many of the gardens, were comparatively late comers. Beeches were widespread, also oaks, hornbeams and ashes. There were many vineyards and winemaking was a profitable industry. The hotel where she was staying was the Taurida, run by Intourist, and Chekhov had once stayed there. She turned to the historical notes, hoping to find something more amusing. Although the Crimean War was what the place was connected with in most British minds, and Sevastopol lay round the corner, it was completely ignored. Recalling the watery miles that she had traversed to reach the peninsular, Venice wondered how long the old sailing ships had taken to do the voyage to Scutari. It must have been an agonising trip for the wretched wounded and it was surprising that any had survived it.

Becoming restless, she wandered about the grounds and found in the courtyard of the hotel the starting point of the cable way leading up to Darsan Hill, a prominent rise in the centre of Yalta. She contemplated it, wondering if she dared make the excursion on her own, for there must be a wonderful view from the top. Deciding it would take too long, she retraced her steps to the terrace which overlooked the Lenin Embankment, a promenade closed to traffic which was thronged with holidaymakers. Watching them a little wistfully, she heard her name called and Kemal came striding towards her.

'Come on,' he called. 'We have the right time to join a bus going to the Livadia Palace. That is somewhere you would like to see, yes?'

'But Selma . . .?' she faltered.

'May not be back for some time. Would you not like to see something while you are here?'

Venice went with alacrity to the entrance of the hotel where a bus was filling up with sightseers.

The Livadia Palace, one-time summer residence of the unfortunate Nicholas Romanoff, last Tsar of Russia, was a long white building with a pillared portico set amidst a garden full of flowers and shrubs. The grounds sloped towards the sea, providing a magnificent view. An old woman in a sackcloth apron was weeding the flower beds.

They went in at the side entrance, where they had to tie over their shoes large flapping pieces of felt, the operation superintended by an autocratic old woman. This precaution was to protect the polished floors of the palace. The place had been turned into a museum, but its chief exhibit was the Conference Room where Stalin, Churchill and Roosevelt planned the last stages of the war. The table at which they had sat was roped off and on the wall beside it was a large painting depicting the famous trio.

'Thank the Supreme power, we were neutral in that war,' Kemal said, as they went back into the sunshine. He glanced at her obliquely. 'We were your enemies in the first one.'

When Mustapha Kemal had defeated the Allies at Gallipoli. She said hastily: 'It's all too long ago to affect me personally.'

From the Livadia they were escorted across a lovely park leading to another and older palace, the Alupka, which had also been turned into a museum. They did not go in, and after giving the huge arched entrance an admiring look, they turned back into the park. The guide came hurrying after them, but Kemal told her Venice was tired and wanted to sit down. Reluctantly she left them to follow the rest of her flock. They found a spot with water amid trees and rocks where swans swam. Far above them through gaps in the foliage they could glimpse the huge barren crags of the mountains which formed a bastion against the northern winds. Kemal indicated a flat-topped rock and Venice sank down upon it with relief, since she was wearing only thin sandals and her feet ached. Kemal sat down beside her and told her:

'We are leaving tonight. I have managed to obtain berths on a Russian ship. She is calling at Odessa on the way back, but I think the rest and sea air will do the Professor good. Also perhaps you would like to see some more of Russia?'

'I should indeed,' Venice said eagerly, 'but can you afford to be so long away?'

'It will complete my convalescence,' he told her, 'already I feel a new man.' He looked about him appreciatively. 'It is beautiful here, yes?'

'An enchanted garden,' Venice murmured dreamily, watching a great white swan go gliding past.

Kemal was watching her face with an inscrutable expression. Her pure profile was etched against the background of dark rock and greenery with cameo clarity. The tree that shaded their rock threw mauve shadows over her white dress and gave mystery to her long eyes.

She wore no hat and stray sunbeams filtering through the leafy shade dusted her pale hair with golden motes.

'Yes, an enchanted garden,' he said softly, 'and you are the fairy princess who rules it.'

Such a flight of fancy from him startled her, and she turned to face him, her eyes wide.

'A very prosaic fairy,' she protested.

'Ah, no.' He shook his head and to her surprise quoted an English poem:

> 'Full beautiful, a faery's child.
> Her hair was long, her step was light,
> And her eyes were wild.'

She met his gaze fixed upon her face; the intent grey eyes held a hidden fire.

'Goodness, fancy you knowing that poem,' she said with an uneasy laugh. 'But I don't like it. Poor Keats was dying of consumption when he wrote it.'

'Pity he could not come to Yalta,' Kem remarked. 'They could have cured him now, but we all have to die some time and he was spared growing old.' He sighed, and went on: 'I had a cosmopolitan education, including a course in English literature, and I admire Keats.' He smiled mischievously and quoted again, 'She looked at me as she did love.' Venice hastily looked away, and he added urgently: 'Do not say anything, keep still and let the magic sink into you.'

Magic there was, the whispering trees, the scent of flowers, the white plumage of the swans and the ardent gaze of the man beside her. It was all wrong, she could never be anything to Kemal or he to her. The gap between them, not the least of which was their different nationalities, was too wide. And there was Bill, awaiting her return, but for these few moments she could dream of what might have been.

As if sensing her thoughts he said:

'There are moments when it is possible to forget the dictates of common sense, the restrictions of normal life and wander in a world of makebelieve, such moments refresh the spirit. We have decided this is an enchanted garden and this is a magic hour.'

Venice was silent as she had been bidden. She had known the man beside her attracted her, but she had resolutely refused to think about him in that context. It was so hopeless, and he knew it too. But there was no harm in stealing these few moments from eternity. For this brief space they were man and woman alone in Eden with perfect accord between them.

Kemal leaned forward and took her face between his hands, sun-tanned, capable, long-fingered hands. For a while he stared deep into her eyes, and afterwards Venice was to wonder with dismay what he read in them. At the time she did not care. His eyes were darkened with the pupils enlarged, and she again saw in them a flickering flame. Then he bent his head and very deliberately kissed her lips. His mouth lingered on hers but was not possessive; his kiss held as much renunciation as passion. A tremor ran through Venice's body, setting her nerves quivering. Gently she raised her hand and stroked the smooth brown head. His hair was soft as silk.

Footsteps and a nasal American voice:

'My, wasn't that swell? It'll be something to tell the folks back home.'

Kemal gave a long sigh and dropped his hands.

'That has broken the spell,' he said with a wry smile. He got to his feet with his lithe feline grace. 'It is time we returned,' he told her, glancing at his watch. 'The coach will be leaving and Cousin Selma will believe we are lost.'

He drew her to her feet, and hand in hand they

walked away from the enchanted garden, outcasts from paradise.

Selma was waiting for them at the Taurida, and was annoyed by their truancy.

'You might have waited for me,' she reproached them.

'There was not time,' Kem told her patiently. 'We only just caught the coach when it was leaving and we did not know when you would be back.'

Selma was staring at Venice with narrowed eyes.

'Something's happened to you,' she announced

Oh lord, Venice thought, have I got stars in my eyes? Yet why should I have them, because this affair is finished before it has begun. Nevertheless she was conscious of an inner exaltation. Kemal, the self-sufficient, the cool aloof observer, had kissed her, he had found her desirable. And herself? Did she love him, or her image of him, for she did not really know him? Was this what was meant by infatuation? All that was certain was that she had never felt like this with Bill; he had been just a good pal and though his touch did not repel her, neither did it thrill her. When Kemal had kissed her she had experienced ecstasy.

Kemal said with admirable aplomb:

'Venice has been transported back into the glories of Imperial Russia, and they have gone to her head. Now we must return to the practical present. We leave tonight.'

This news diverted Selma, who demanded how, when and where. Venice left them together going up to the room reserved for her, in which apparently she would not be sleeping. She wanted to be alone to relive those magical moments that could never be repeated.

They left Yalta in the pall of a purple dusk pierced by the sparkle of a myriad lights from the buildings above the quayside and stretching far up the hills. As the ship headed out into the Black Sea, Venice stood at the rail watching the night swallow the dim shapes of the mountain crests, and the lights recede. She would never forget Yalta.

If Yalta was a holiday paradise, Odessa was all practical purpose. Their ship sailed into its immense harbour next morning, where craft of many nations large and small were loading and unloading, and the entrance was guarded by gunboats. The Professor shared a cabin with Kemal, the two girls another one. The ship was much smaller than the cruise liner that had brought them to Russia, and not so luxuriously fitted. The passengers were mostly Russians, some of whom were returning from convalescence at Yalta, and there was a nurse on board. She insisted upon examining Lucas Hadleigh next morning, much to his disgust, and pronounced him fit and in no need of her further attention.

'Do not forget that the Soviet Union has saved and cured you,' she told him. 'And discharged you in good health.'

'I'll be eternally grateful to that great country,' he returned politely, adding as soon as she had gone, 'but there was nothing wrong with me.'

As they would not be sailing until after lunch, Kemal and the two girls joined an expedition going ashore. The Professor, who had seen the town before, preferred to remain on board.

Selma had adopted a proprietorial attitude towards Kem. Although she had said nothing, Venice sensed that she resented her expedition with him to the palace and was seeking to assert her claim to his undivided attention. Until she had decided which if either of the Osman brothers she wished to marry, she considered they were her preserve. So in the coach she sat beside him, relegating Venice to the seat behind them, which she shared with a lady whose nationality she never discovered, since she maintained a frozen silence throughout the trip.

Odessa is a fine town with wide tree-lined streets, decorated with imposing pieces of modern statuary. The coach stopped above the Potemkin steps, scene of the mutiny, and they all got out. Selma clung to Kem's arm, as if she needed his support, and he shot an apologetic glance at Venice with a shrug of his shoulders.

'Have you become the clinging vine, cousin?' he asked Selma.

She smiled archly. 'Strong men like you were made to prop up feminine weakness; doesn't it give your ego a boost?'

Venice did not hear his reply, but he did not look appreciative.

After the hurly-burly of Istanbul the streets seemed quiet, almost deserted, with a noticeable absence of private cars. The average Russian cannot afford a car, which are prohibitive in price. Venice looked with interest at the women shoppers, who for the most part did not wear trousers and were stout and homely. A few had hair dyed with the unmistakable hue of henna. The realisation that she was standing upon Russian soil suddenly overwhelmed her. She had never imagined she would actually visit that notable country.

Back in the coach their guide rattled off the prescribed information at intervals. Kem nudged a bored Selma.

'Listen to this. As you're a teacher it should interest you.'

They were being told that Odessa contained many universities, and several were pointed out to them. Children went to school at seven and must attend for ten years. The year was divided into two terms, and children were graded according to ability. Those who reached the required standard went on to university and work was guaranteed for all students.

'What's so wonderful about that?' Selma demanded. 'And I'm on holiday.'

'But holidays have to end,' he told her. 'Their purpose is to renew us for the activities ahead.'

Venice wondered if he were hinting that Selma would be expected to use her training. That, she knew, was not her friend's idea at all. Surely she must realise that Kem was too serious to suit her and that Ahmet would be a better proposition? As for her own future, that was represented by Bill, unless she wanted to die an old maid. The episode in the garden at Yalta had no connection with reality, already it had become like a dream. Kem had merely succumbed to a moment's relaxation, and though she was more sympathetic towards his aims than Selma, he would not regard an English wife as an asset on his upward climb to attain his ambitions. Occasionally as they descended from the coach to view various monuments, including a huge statue of Lenin erected before a municipal block in an open square, she caught his eyes upon her with an enigmatical expression and wondered if he were recalling those magical moments. Was it love that had flowered between them? But she doubted that he had any deep feeling for her, and she was not sure if her own towards him were strong enough to justify attempting to bridge the gulf between them. Certainly he would not help her to do that.

The ship left Odessa as soon as they had returned for lunch, and continued its voyage across the Black Sea. Selma, although she knew no Russian, managed to make her usual impact on the crew. Once Venice overheard her father scolding her:

'You mustn't be so free, my dear if you hope to be a respected Turkish wife.'

'Respected fiddlesticks,' Selma retorted scornfully. 'Ahmet understands. He knows what the modern world is like.'

Venice did not hear the Professor's rejoinder as she hastily moved out of earshot, but she felt a quite disproportionate surge of relief.

In material substance there was no difference between the brothers, both inheriting equal parts of their father's estate. The Bosphorus house belonged to Zubeyde and would come to Ahmet; Kem had one in Ankara, but in temperament there was a great deal of difference, and Ahmet's shallow nature and liking for frivolity was obviously more suited to Selma than Kem's earnest aspirations, which she could never share. But it was no concern of hers which brother Selma chose, Venice reminded herself. Soon she would be returning to England and it was unlikely she would meet the Osmans again. Bill would be eagerly awaiting her return. Eagerly? That was hardly the right word. He took her very much for granted, and she was beginning to wonder if she could bring herself to marry him. She knew now that she did not love him and doubted that the affection she felt for him was enough. This thing with Kem would fade when she had left his vicinity; it could not be lasting after so short a while. Infatuation, she told herself angrily, because he's so different from anyone I've ever known, and I've mixed him up with Ataturk whom I admire tremendously. But deep down in the centre of her being she felt it was much more.

The ship approached the Bosphorus on their last night at sea. It would dock in the small hours at Uskadur, the modern name for Scutari, but they were told they would not have to disembark until after breakfast, as the ship would be some hours unloading cargo.

After dinner, Venice stood on the afterdeck watching the churning wake which left a frothy trail across the water. Seagulls screeched over the debris thrown overboard, the advent of the birds a sure sign that land was near. Dusk had fallen and a few stars shone. From the depths of the ship came the sound of a balalaika band; the off-duty crew were entertaining the few passengers.

She knew he was there before she saw him, though his rubber-soled sandals made no sound on the deck. He came up beside her and laid his hands next to hers on the rail. In every nerve she was aware of him. For some while neither spoke, their silence a closer intimacy than any words, until unable to bear it any longer, Venice remarked that they would soon be home, an observation that by its very triteness restored them to commonplace.

'It has been a successful trip, yes?' he commented, his brooding gaze fixed on the sea.

'Very pleasant.'

'Pleasant?' He sounded mocking.

'Well, what would you call it?'

'A revelation.'

'And what do you mean by that?'

He placed his long nervous hand over hers on the deck rail.

'You know what I mean. We became known to each other.'

A thrill shot through her at his touch, with all her being she yearned for his embrace, and she said stonily:

'There's no future for us, is there?'

His fingers tightened over hers. 'No, and I am glad that you understand that, Venice.'

Rebellion against the fate that had entrapped them surged up in her.

'Oh, why,' she whispered in a low quivering voice, 'did it have to be you?'

He shrugged slightly. 'Kismet.' He took hold of her wrist and turned her to face him. Their features were blurred in the dim light, and he was only a dark shape in front of her, but he still held her wrist and his fingers were warm and vital.

'A marriage between us would be suicide for me and madness for you,' he told her quietly.

Venice experienced a shock to realise that he had actually considered marriage, something that she had not yet done, but as he said, it would be madness. She could not accept an alien way of life, even for him ... or could she? She caught her breath; the vista the thought opened before her was alluring.

'Sweet madness,' she whispered.

'Yes, but not to be contemplated.' Intuitively she knew that he was fighting his own impulses. 'Is there not another man in England who has spoken for you?'

'Oh no, he hasn't,' she exclaimed quickly, smiling at his way of putting it. 'We're not engaged and I doubt we ever will be ... now. I don't love him, Kem.'

'Many marriages are contracted without this thing called love. They are usually quite satisfactory.'

She said bluntly: 'Do you want me to marry him?'

His hold on her wrist tightened to a painful grip.

'I want what is best for you,' he returned.

'But poor Bill would be very much second best,' she protested. A gleam of mischief came into her eyes, but it was too dark for him to see it. 'At Yalta you told the authorities I was your fiancée. Aren't you afraid of being compromised?'

'It is understood it was only an expedient,' he assured her hastily. Then he sighed. 'Though I wish it had been true.'

Very softly she murmured: 'Are you certain it's so impossible?'

'Yes.' He dropped her wrist and turned to the rail. 'Different customs, different faiths,' he said harshly.

Venice was silent, her eyes fixed yearningly on his well shaped head, black against the lighter darkness of the sky. She knew that in the gardens at Yalta she had betrayed herself, knew also he was not prepared to find a place for her in his life, that the barriers between them were too high to scale. Venice Franklin would be an impediment in his upward climb, and what would she do with herself in Ankara? Every tenet of reason and common sense showed that they must part ... and yet ...

Kem turned from the rail with a sound like a groan and took her into his arms.

'Oh, Venice,' he sighed, and murmured endearments in his own language.

A tide of intense emotion surged through Venice's veins. Her body became limp in his arms. Impelled by the urgency of her desire, she whispered: 'I can't bear to leave you. Take me with you to Ankara.'

She felt his muscles tense and wondered if he had understood her. What was the advantage of belonging to a permissive age if one could not be permissive, when it was so desperately important to her? His hold tightened so that she could hardly breathe, then slowly relaxed.

'It is impossible, darling,' he said thickly. 'I am a public figure there, nor could I bear to have mud slung at you. Then there is the Professor Bey, he would think I had abused his friendship—you are in his care, yes?'

'No. I'm of age and responsible for my own acts.' But her crazy impulse was dying, to be replaced by a dull misery. 'I was mad for a moment.'

'Sweet madness,' he said gently, repeating her own

words, 'but I would be a villain to take advantage of it.'

Venice wound her arms about his neck, clinging to him.

'It's hard,' she whispered.

'I know. You must go away and forget me.'

But he still held her close as if defying the spectre of parting.

'I'll be going home soon, but I'll never forget you as long as I live,' Venice murmured.

'Oh, foolish one,' he chided her gently. 'You must not spoil your life because you have met me.'

'You haven't spoilt it, you've enriched it,' she declared bravely.

But for the moment he was hers and she was in his arms. They stood interlocked in the quiet darkness, their emotion all the more intense because it must be denied fulfilment.

'Ven!'

They started apart at the sound of Selma's outraged voice. She had come upon them unperceived and had been staring at their entwined figures in horrified unbelief. 'Oh, how could you?' she cried reproachfully. 'Ven, how can you behave like this!'

CHAPTER SIX

SELMA'S query shocked Venice back to sanity. How could she? A good question. She, who had always prided herself upon her fastidiousness and being level-headed, had been prepared to pursue a course of action that would have been the height of folly, and had been checked, not by her own good sense, but Kem's. She had never in her wildest fantasies imagined she was the type of woman who would lose all for love, to use a hackneyed expression, and she was not even sure that what was between her and Kem was love, it had come about so suddenly, but if he had asked her she would have willingly followed him barefoot across the world, such was the strength of her infatuation. But he had demanded no such sacrifice from her, only the more painful one of sundering herself from him.

While she hesitated wondering how to excuse herself to Selma, Kem offered his own explanation.

'You have ... what do you say ... caught me out,' he said ruefully. He moved towards the other girl. 'I can only assure you that Venice was not to blame. I am only human and finding myself alone with a pretty girl on a summer night, I ... er ... forgot myself.' He turned back to Venice. 'Forgive me, Venice Hanim, I behaved unpardonably.'

Though she knew he was trying to protect her, Venice felt as though he had thrown a pail of cold water over her, he sounded so convincing. It darted through her mind that perhaps that was all it had been to him, an opportunity, a willing girl and the drive of his sensual impulses. The poignancy she had sensed behind his renunciation had only existed in her imagination.

'Oh, I know what men are,' Selma returned caustically. 'They're all the same and you're no exception, but I can't get over Ven ... Ven of all people to be necking in the dark!' She advanced towards Venice's shadowy figure. 'I always believed you were above such low behaviour, Ven, I respected you for it, though I know I don't follow your example myself'—she giggled selfconsciously—'I'm too warm-blooded and men won't leave me alone. But you're quite different, and what about Bill?'

This speech stung Venice with its subtle implications that she was frigid, men did not find her attractive and she was being unfaithful to Bill. She retorted drily:

'He's probably doing the same thing with some hefty Amazon. He's free to do as he pleases—we made no promises.'

'Surely you malign him, you were so devoted to each other,' Selma insisted for Kem's benefit.

'You read more into the situation than existed,' Venice flashed, wanting to dismiss the subject of Bill. She was painfully aware of Kem's presence beside her in the dark, so near yet divided.

'But you gave me to understand ...' Selma was beginning, when Kem intervened tactfully:

'If you ladies want to get any sleep you had better go below. We shall reach port before long.'

Low on the horizon the lights on land were throwing a glow into the sky.

'I'm going.' Venice moved away across the deck. 'Goodnight, Kem.' She reached the companionway and stumbled down it, nearly missing her footing in a turmoil of mixed emotions. Oh, why had Selma had to come and spoil their last moments together?

The cabin she shared with Selma was much smaller

than the one they had had on the cruise liner, and was fitted with two berths, one above the other. Selma had chosen the upper one. It was on the outside of the ship, so it did possess a porthole, an amenity for which they were grateful. Venice sat down on her bunk and began mechanically to undress, a merciful numbness creeping over her. She wondered vaguely what Selma was saying to Kem—nothing complimentary about herself, she could be sure, and he ... perhaps he had been glad of the interruption, since he had said all he had to say. Men, unlike women, never wanted to prolong goodbyes, and he had insisted it was farewell.

Selma came in when Venice was in her pyjamas, her dark eyes sparkling irefully.

'You're nuts,' she said succinctly.

'Probably,' Venice agreed wearily. 'But is that your business?'

'Of course it is.' Selma turned to the small mirror above the dressing shelf and began to loosen her hair. 'I introduced you to the Osmans and you yourself warned me they were foreigners. You should know as well as I do that their manners and traditions are different from ours. What Kem must think of you I don't like to consider.' She swung round and surveyed her friend critically. Venice's hair hung in a silver-gilt cloud over her shoulders, her face was pale and a little strained. 'I suppose you attract him because you're so fair,' she admitted grudgingly. 'But he isn't safe to play with, for all his aloof airs, and if you're too forward, he'll take advantage of it.'

'Kem's not like that,' Venice said, quick to defend him.

'Then what did you think you were doing? Surely you know that if he marries anybody it'll be me.'

'But you prefer Ahmet?' Venice asked anxiously.

'That drip! He isn't half the man Kem is,' Selma

declared. She turned back to study her own face in the glass. 'Please give me credit for a little discernment. It'll have to be Kem.'

Venice stared at her in dismay. 'So you've decided?'

'More or less.' Selma started to cream her face. 'I find Kem exciting. It'll be fun breaking down that icy reserve of his, and as you've probably discovered, there's plenty of fire underneath.'

Venice stood up and went to look out of the porthole. The rays from the lighthouse at the entrance to the Bosphorus were splintering the dark. She was very much afraid that her own actions had drawn Selma towards Kem. Her affection for herself could not stand up to rivalry for a man's favour. She took it as her prerogative to annex any male admiration within reach. That Kem had found Venice attractive was enough to spur her on to conquer him. But she was swayed by her moods and once she came again within Ahmet's orbit, she might change her mind. If she did not, Venice was sure the result would be disaster. She was not the right sort of wife for Kem.

'Do you love him?' she asked quietly, for that might redeem the situation. She had reason to believe that Kem did not love Selma, but if she were meek and affectionate he might come to do so.

Selma laughed. 'I'm not one for the love eternal, till death do us part nonsense,' she said lightly. 'If we don't make a go of it, I believe divorce here is easy.'

Venice turned round and regarded her friend sadly.

'Doesn't seem to me you're going about it in quite the right spirit,' she observed drily. 'I suppose he will be agreeable?'

'But of course, he'll gain very definite advantages,' Selma declared smugly. She gave Venice a contrite glance. 'I'm sorry to break up your little romance, darling, but it's best to face facts, and an affair between you and him would be most unsuitable.'

'Quite, but would you mind if he loves someone else?'

'Who else is there?' Selma stared at Venice challengingly. 'Darling, you must get this into your head, Kem would never, never consider marrying you.' Venice winced. 'He couldn't even pretend that you were Turkish and once he's sure I'm available he'll not give you another thought. I mean ... dash it all ... who would look at you when he could have me?'

'Who indeed?' Venice echoed, gazing at Selma's rich beauty, but Kem had never paid Selma much attention, and Venice recalled that Ahmet had said he found her own looks more original, so it was just possible that Kem was of the same opinion. Not that it made any difference, the dice were too heavily loaded against her.

'Will you mind living in Ankara?' she asked.

'Why should I? I believe it's quite a modern town now, and of course I can always fly over to Istanbul if I get bored while Kem's engaged with his stuffy civic duties. Perhaps I can persuade him to resign, we'll have money enough, and live the life of a man of leisure. That would be much more amusing.'

Venice stared at her in wonderment. How little Selma knew Kem! Something in her despondent attitude came through to Selma, for she came away from the mirror and put her arm round her friend's shoulders.

'Darling, you aren't really hurt, are you?' she asked anxiously. 'You know Kem was only amusing himself when he took you out and I was tied up with Pa. He couldn't mean anything serious, surely you don't imagine that he did?'

'I've always known there couldn't be anything serious between us.' Venice assured her.

'Then that's all right,' Selma gave a sigh of relief

and continued with her toilet. 'Don't you know Kem is all for Turkey for the Turks? It's a good thing I take after my mother, or he might jib even at me. Haven't you noticed a likeness between me and Zubeyde? Oh, not only physically, I've also got her indolent voluptous temperament that conceals the iron hand in the velvet glove.' She giggled. 'The favourites in the seraglios knew how to get round the Sultan, and I'll get my own way with Kem.'

'But Kem isn't in the least like those old sultans,' Venice protested. 'Most of them were dreadful people.'

'You don't know, and I'm sure he can be pretty ruthless at times,' Selma declared. 'But I understand him—it's hereditary instinct.'

Venice thought that she was being optimistic. She did not doubt Kem's ruthlessness, he had been so with herself, but he would no more yield to Selma's pleadings than to her own. His mind was fixed upon his objective and no woman would be allowed to thwart him. She prayed passionately that he would realise Selma's incompatibility before it was too late. Apparently he was not yet committed, and that was comforting. She would hate to think he had not been a free man when he had embraced her upon deck.

Selma gave her a kiss, climbed into the upper berth and immediately fell asleep. But Venice lay wakeful in the lower one, the events of the evening going round and round in her brain. Selma called Kem cold and ruthless, but he had shown her a different side of himself; he could be tender, imaginative even poetical. Though he had declared they had no future, and Selma had decided to annex him, Venice could not entirely give up hope. It was yet to be seen if he would accept Selma, and were the obstacles he had mentioned really so insurmountable? Although Selma's insistence that he had only been amusing himself with her had raised doubts, in her heart she still believed that her passion was reciprocated.

There was still time for him to reflect, she would be around for a while yet, and he might recall that Lucas Hadleigh at risk of prejudicing his career had married a Turk and been happy with her, and he knew that many Turks working abroad had brought home foreign brides. Or was her nationality an excuse to repudiate her because his feelings for her were not strong enough to risk a marriage or even a liaison? She flushed in the dark as she had remembered that she had recklessly hinted that she would accept less than a legitimate bond. But she had nothing to lose—except him. She could have gone to Ankara on the pretext of seeking for a position as a teacher of English there and no one would have been any the wiser. But he had preferred that she should go back to England, where they would never meet again.

Venice moved restlessly in her narrow bed, faced with the truth that his scruples had been stronger than his desire. She ought to feel honoured that he would not consider her lightly, but she did not, she only felt bereft. Then it occurred to her that if he were considering marrying Selma he would obviously have to sever all connection with herself, but he had given no indication that he had any expectation of doing so, gilded though Selma was. She had the impression that he rather despised her friend. Surely then he would never descend to a mercenary marriage with her? It would be more reprehensible than if she married Bill.

Bill. She would have to break with him now she had come to recognise how superficial their relationship was. Since coming to Istanbul she had far outgrown it, nor did she think he would find her difficult to replace. There had never been any depth of emotion involved, they were merely two young people who had found each other's company congenial, and she doubted that would be so any longer.

If Kemal did not relent, the prospect for the future was bleak. No Hadleighs, no Bill and worst of all no Kem, for she would not dare to visit Istanbul again if he married someone else. All she would have was her Aunt Joan who had never wanted her and never showed her any affection. She would be alone in the world—but, she thought, she had had a good education, was healthy and not bad looking. So many people had much less, she ought to be able to make something of her life without repining. It was said that when one door shut another opened, and she hoped one would open soon, so many doors seemed to have closed, this last one with a bang.

So the long night hours crawled by while she wrestled with hope and despair, and the first light found her still open-eyed and restless. She knew by the sounds outside that the ship had docked.

She got up and dressed, moving quietly so as not to disturb Selma, packed her few belongings and went up on deck. It was only a few days since she had set forth for Yalta, but a century seemed to have elapsed since she had last seen the Bosphorus. The first flush of sunlight gilded the buildings across the water, the now familiar shapes of mosques and minarets along the skyline. Uskudar port was packed with buildings and had its own share of mosques. Already the ferryboats were plying across the three waters, Marmara, the Bosphorus and the Golden Horn which the Turks call Halic. Venice's spirits rose; she was lucky to be here, fortunate to be enjoying such a wonderful experience; even her love for Kem had widened her horizon, taught her a great deal she had not known about herself, and there had been moments which would become treasured memories to look back upon when she was aged.

An old tag recurred to her: 'It is better to have loved and lost than never to have loved at all.' But there was still a possibility that she had not lost after all.

Selma came hurrying up on deck at an unwontedly early hour. Venice suspected ironically that she had feared she had had another rendezvous with Kem. She was transparently relieved to find Venice alone, which rather gave the lie to her insistence the night before that Kemal was not interested in Venice. Of him there was no sign and when they went below to breakfast, Professor Hadleigh told them he had already left for his offices across the water. Both girls were disappointed, Selma because she was anxious to start subjugating him, and Venice because she wanted to see how a night's reflection had affected him; he might have decided to relent.

The Professor told them that they would take the ferry across the water and then a taxi for the Ciragan Caddesi.

'Zubeyde Hanim will send the rest of your things over to the Villa Yasmin,' he told them, 'and we shall be able to start your holiday properly.' He looked with concern at Venice's pale face and heavy eyes. 'It's obvious you haven't slept, my dear—perhaps you found your cabin stuffy. You'll be able to have a good rest once we're settled in at the Villa Yasmin.'

The villa was not as luxurious as the Osmans' house and its furniture was conventionally English; also it was much noisier, lacking the convenience of an enclosed courtyard. Instead there was a terrace in front of it, over which an awning could be drawn in the daytime. On it was set out the usual array of canvas chairs and loungers. The servants, a married couple, were there to greet them, the local grapevine having apprised them that the master was on his way back. Venice had a room upstairs looking towards the Bosphorus, and worn out with conjectures and emotions, she slept for most of the day, only coming down for dinner.

The next morning Ahmet turned up with a new sports car he had just bought and asked Selma to come out with him.

'I would include you,' he said politely to Venice, 'but the back seat is not very comfortable, it will only accommodate one person sitting sideways. Perhaps another time?'

'Oh, don't bother about me.' Venice was a little abrupt, she did not want any gallantries from Ahmet. 'I'm not keen on sports cars anyway.'

'But that is extraordinary.' He grinned maliciously. 'Sure it is not a case of sour grapes?'

'Oh, come on,' Selma cried impatiently, 'Ven hasn't got over Yalta yet. She went sightseeing with Kem and it exhausted her.' Her expression was nearly as malicious as Ahmet's.

'Lucky Kem,' Ahmet ejaculated, 'so he has been making the running.' He winked audaciously at Venice.

'Oh, don't be so absurd,' Selma told him crossly.

They departed in a cloud of dust, and the Professor turned to Venice and asked to be excused for an hour, as he had to go across and see Zubeyde and thank her for her care of the girls.

'Unless you'd like to come with me?' he enquired.

Venice declined. Sometime she supposed she would have to tender her own thanks to Zubeyde, but not yet; she did not want Kem to think she was pursuing him. He probably was not at home, but she would prefer not to risk encountering him. If he wanted to see her, he knew where she was.

So she settled herself on a lounger on the terrace with a book, and presently she had a visitor. One of the doves from next door flew down on to the paving at her feet and eyed her inquisitively. She liked to think that it had recognised her, and when it fluttered up on to the arm rest of her chair, she was sure it had. She kept quite still while its ruby eyes peered this way and that, then having ascertained that there was nothing edible within reach, it flew away.

Venice opened her book and closed it again. If Kem gave no sign she ought to go back to England, for Selma's manner was becoming hostile and she did not want to attract any attentions from Ahmet. She supposed she could change her ticket to an earlier flight; she might get a cancellation if she were lucky. Later she would take a bus into Istanbul and consult a travel agency. At the moment she felt too languid to move. Presently she dozed.

She awoke with the sense of being watched and rubbing her eyes looked about her dazedly. Kemal was standing leaning negligently against the wall of the house, hands in the pockets of his trousers, watching her with an unusual softness of expression.

'Oh!' She smoothed her hair with a self-conscious gesture. 'I must have been asleep.'

'You were, and I was tempted to awaken you in the traditional manner.'

He had come to her and his coming could only mean one thing. She looked up at him with all her heart in her eyes, as she said simply: 'Why didn't you?' and raised her face expectantly.

He started towards her, but checked before he reached her. His face became expressionless and she sensed his withdrawal.

'Selma is out,' she told him mechanically. 'There's no one here but me.'

'I know. I came because I had to speak to you alone.' He hesitated. 'I have something to tell you.'

The momentary chill that had touched her when he had halted was instantly dispelled, and her heart began to beat fast with joyful anticipation. He had come to tell her that he had changed his mind, that he could not do without her, that their love would overcome all obstacles.

'Yes?' she prompted eagerly as he paused.

He looked straight into her eyes, his as hard and cold as steel.

'I felt it only fair to tell you at once that I have asked the Professor Bey for his daughter's hand in marriage and tonight we shall announce our betrothal.'

His words came curt and clipped, his face was like granite without any sign of feeling. Venice was stunned, her lips moved soundlessly, but she could not speak. This was the final death of hope. As her face slowly whitened, Kem turned away, unwilling to witness her reaction. He continued harshly:

'My stepmother and Selma's father have been urging me to take Selma Hanim to wife, even before she came out here. The union will consolidate our joint business ventures, and the Professor Bey is prepared to make generous settlements. Also she will be his heir. He applied for naturalisation some time ago and will soon be one of us officially. Selma will of course become so. The money will be of assistance to my impoverished country. I have no option.'

Slowly Venice emerged from the state of shock his words had produced. She ought to have expected no less. What Selma had said in the cabin should have prepared her for the inevitable, but she had not anticipated that it would happen so soon, not until she was back in England, if at all. Then she remembered something. Kemal could not know that Selma had gone out with Ahmet; she might have already changed her mind.

'Aren't you reckoning without Selma?' she asked. 'She isn't here. She's with Ahmet.'

'That was arranged so that I could speak with Zubeyde and the Professor without interruption.'

'I see, and also to be able to tell me of your deliberations,' she said bitterly. 'Thank you for bringing me the good news. Am I expected to rejoice ... for your country's sake or for yours?'

Without waiting for his reply, she swung herself with a supple movement off the canvas lounger and walked unsteadily to the edge of the terrace, leaning against the balustrade for support. She stared unseeingly at the sunlit water. She had the vague feeling that something beautiful had died.

'Venice,' Kem said gently from behind her, and the compassion in his voice stung her pride.

'Actually I had had warning of your intentions,' she said dully. 'But I found them hard to credit, after ... after what happened ...' She broke off. Better not to remind him of those moments on the boat deck. In justice to him she must admit he never had made her any promises, he had always told her their love was hopeless. Love? Had he ever mentioned love? 'But I thought ...' she went on, and stopped again. What had she thought? That Kem out of consideration for her feelings would delay in snatching such a prize? That he would have second thoughts about letting her go? Of course he would not; he was no Romeo to lose all for passion's sake, but a hard, calculating man who seized his opportunities. She doubted he was even capable of true love. All she had been to him was a passing fancy to be cajoled with pretty phrases and a few kisses, and cast aside when it was expedient to do so.

'Venice,' he said again, 'believe me, I am sorry. I hate to cause you pain.'

Perhaps he did, but he was not the one who was suffering. She had betrayed her feelings to him and so he was offering her compassion—a poor exchange. She swung round to face him, her green eyes glittering in her pale face. She did not want his pity.

'Don't distress yourself,' she said sharply. 'I'll soon get over it—you were just a holiday romance. We English girls expect them when we go abroad as part of the vacation. There's a little sentimental nostalgia, and then, pouf! it's all forgotten until next year.' Desperately she strove to make her tone light, but there was a brittle edge to it. If only he would go away, not stand there looking so devastatingly attractive in his blue tee-shirt and cream-coloured slacks, slight and supple, yet exuding the energy and forcefulness that made him so irresistible. She drew her hand across her brow as if to expel his image.

'I assure you there's no real harm done,' she went on feverishly, knowing she was babbling but unable to stop. 'How could there be when I've only known you for such a short time? You've done very well for yourself. Selma is beautiful, rich and half Turkish, you'll have everything. I . . . I must congratulate you.'

'Venice, stop it!' He took her by the shoulders and shook her. 'I have not got everything, as you put it, and if you think this is easy for me . . .'

'Please, Kem, don't try to salve my feelings with soft soap,' she interrupted. 'I understand your position perfectly. You never have held out any hope for me . . . for us. I . . . I do sincerely wish you happiness.'

'Happiness!' he echoed, dropping his hands from her shoulders. He stepped back to widen the distance between them. 'That is not my aim, as you should know. My personal desires are of no account.'

'So noble and public-spirited!' A mocking note crept into her voice. 'You're hard as marble, aren't you,

Kem? Nothing can divert you from the course you've set yourself.'

She remembered that Selma had said he could be ruthless, and so he was.

Kem did not contradict her, his mouth was set in a line of grim determination, but his grey eyes met her stormy ones with a plea for understanding. Venice's brittle composure suddenly snapped, her precarious control crumbling away. He was so dear and so implacable.

'Oh, Kem,' she cried brokenly, 'I would follow you to the ends of the earth barefoot. I would welcome poverty and hardship if I could share them with you, I ... I'd give my life for you, but that's not enough, is it? I can in no way benefit your country, and I come between you and your ambition, so you can't find even a corner for me in your life. I must be pushed aside ... forgotten ...'

She looked beautiful in her distress, her eyes like emeralds, her face delicately flushed, her hair a silver-gilt nimbus about her head. Kem made an inarticulate sound and took a stride towards her, drawn by her passion, with a sudden flame leaping in his eyes. Venice drew a quick breath, anticipating his embrace; at last she had shaken him out of his frozen calm. She stretched out her arms towards him, her whole being surrendering to him in a surge of love and longing.

He did not touch her, he halted before he reached her, and put his hand over his eyes with a groan.

'Venice, in the name of Allah say no more.'

Slowly her arms sank to her sides. His words had hit her like a blow with their reminder of the gulf between them. She had forgotten he belonged to the East. She turned away, biting her lips, wishing she could recall her reckless outburst. Not that it mattered, nothing could matter any more. As her emotion ebbed she regained command of herself, and forcing herself to face him, she said quietly:

'I'm sorry. That was pure melodrama. Forget it, please.'

A sweet elusive smile momentarily softened his set face.

'That is impossible. I could never forget such a charming confession.'

Venice winced. All she had done was to flatter his vanity, when she had meant to shame him. She told him hastily:

'I spoke wildly, I ... I didn't know what I was saying.' She pulled herself together with a great effort. The animation died out of her face, the light from her eyes; she looked pale and pinched, insignificant. 'I shall return to England as soon as I can,' she went on calmly. 'I shall take up my old life again where it left off and soon all this will seem like a dream.'

She would become the schoolmarm for which she was destined, teaching other people's children, but she would never have any of her own. Marriage to anyone else was unthinkable now that she had lost Kem.

Silence fell between them. Above the muted sound of the traffic below them, Venice could hear clearly audible the murmuring of the doves in the Osmans' courtyard, a melancholy sound that moved her painfully. If she could avoid it she must never enter that courtyard again. Why did not Kem go? They had said all that could be said, herself rather more than was necessary. She both longed for his departure and yearned for him to stay. They would never be alone together again.

Then at last he spoke, very gently and sadly.

'It is only to be expected that you should think badly of me. I have not treated you well, my darling, and I pray you will pardon me for the hurt I have caused you.'

The endearment brought the smart of tears to her eyes, but she would not let them fall in front of him. Fighting them back, she said distractedly:

'There's nothing to forgive.' She laughed a little wildly. 'We've had some pleasant moments for which I should thank you. I . . . I'll be glad to see old Bill again. He'll be back by the time I get to London.'

In one swift stride Kemal was at her side.

'You will not marry him?'

'I expect so.' Her eyes glinted up at him. 'Why not?'

'You said you did not love him.'

Jealously he gathered her into his arms. She could not meet the intensity of his grey gaze, and she quivered in his hold, but she said steadily:

'Is that any of your business . . . now?'

He was silent for some moments, his hands moving caressingly over her back, then with a sigh he released her.

'No. You are right, it is not.' He pulled out his handkerchief and wiped his forehead. 'Again I must ask for your forgiveness, but the thought of another man . . .' He broke off without completing his sentence.

Venice watched him with a dreary triumph, savouring his jealousy, an emotion that can be so much stronger than love. He was not looking at her and her eyes dwelt yearningly on the lean brown face she loved so well. At least she had lost her heart to no mean man. He would go far, perhaps make history as the great man for whom he had been named had done. He raised his eyes and caught her glance. She said tartly:

'You can't expect me to live like a nun for the rest of my life mulling over impossible might-have-beens.'

'I do not.' He had regained command of himself, and his face was stony. 'I am not the . . . what you say . . . dog in the manger. I wish you every happiness, and he is a lucky fellow.'

Poor Bill, Venice thought, I'm using him as a smoke screen, but he'll never know that.

Kemal glanced at his watch.

'I must go. I have as usual business to attend to. My time is never my own.' He looked at her wistfully. 'It is hard to leave you, fairy's child.'

'Ah no!' Venice cried protestingly. She could not bear to be reminded of that enchanted day at Yalta, at least not yet. She would recall it nostalgically when her heart was less sore, but for the moment it hurt too much.

Kem's eyes moved over her, taking in every detail of her slight, almost childish body, the tendrils of her pale gold hair framing the delicacy of her features, her long green eyes, as if he were trying to impress her image upon his memory for all time. She knew he was taking his farewell of her, and if they met again it would be as strangers. After today he would dismiss her as a charming interlude and fix his mind upon more important affairs, the things that really mattered to him and which she could not share.

'To me you will always be that entrancing lady,' he said gravely. He caught her hand and lifted her unresponsive fingers to his lips. 'Allah go with you.'

Then he was gone, so swiftly that she had no time to make any rejoinder.

The bright day seemed to have darkened around her. Venice walked blindly into the house and sought her own room, thankful that Selma was out. She lay in dumb misery upon her bed, unable to weep, for her sense of loss went too deep for tears. Later she would have to face the Hadleighs with apparent indifference, but for the moment she could indulge her grief.

CHAPTER SEVEN

ORIGINALLY Venice had been expected to stay with the Hadleighs for about a month, unless she received a summons to an interview for a job. As none had come for her she had no pretext for returning to London, and Selma, having obtained what she wanted, reverted to being her old affectionate self.

Bill wrote to tell her that he had decided to extend his holiday so that he would be back about the same time as she was, thereby undermining her possible excuse. The situation was eased by the departure of Kem for Ankara, and Ahmet went away on a business course to Germany. Zubeyde was no fool and having gauged Selma's temperament intended to keep him out of the way until she was safely married. She did not approve of the Professor's daughter's modern manners and would prefer a more conventional bride for her own son. Kemal presumably knew what he was doing and being older than his half-brother was more capable of keeping a flighty young woman in order. Lucas Hadleigh was, she considered, far too lax where Selma was concerned, and with Kemal away she would have every opportunity to get into mischief.

Venice still felt that her presence was an embarrassment, but when Selma heard her ask the Professor for the address of a travel agency she immediately demanded for what, and vehemently opposed her friend's intention of leaving Turkey.

'With Bill still away, you've no one in London except that dreary aunt of yours,' she pointed out. 'Do stay a bit longer, Ven, you've hardly seen anything yet.'

She looked shrewdly at Venice's pale face and shadowed eyes. 'Do you want to go because I was so nasty about Kem?' she asked with disarming candour. 'Please forgive me for that, you know how my tongue runs away with me when I'm upset, and I'm truly sorry. He's gone now, and I do really want you to stay here.'

She had persuaded herself that there could not have been anything serious between Venice and Kem, beyond a mild flirtation. Venice was so sensible and she must know how unsuitable any connection with him would be, and she could not have become attached to him in so short a time.

Venice herself wondered about that. She had always scoffed at the notion of love at first sight, but she could not deny that there had been an inexplicable empathy between herself and the young Turk from the time they had first met, a natural affinity, almost a recognition of someone she had known in a previous existence. Even such a far-fetched possibility was not too bizarre to account for the sudden blaze of emotion that had flared up in her, for she had never even in her teenage years been given to crushes. She had been too repressed, which perhaps was why when her heart was for the first time wholly involved the result had been so devastating. She hoped that if they had met in the past their story would have had a happier ending. Nor was her fancy totally absurd in a part of the world where so many people believed in reincarnation.

Selma continued to badger her to stay.

'With Kem and Ahmet away, I'll be so lonely with only Pa to talk to,' she pleaded. 'And he's always immersed in his books and maps. Zubeyde's so stuffy she'll complain to him if I go about alone. Please stay, Ven, we mayn't ever have another holiday together.'

Venice allowed herself to be persuaded, ashamed to admit that it was the state of her feelings that urged her to flee and the fear that Kem might return before her vacation was up. But she knew he would avoid her if he did, and after one visit to Zubeyde to thank her for her hospitality, a visit that had been an ordeal for her in a house so redolent of Kem's presence, that good lady had not extended any further invitations. Presumably she had decided that the fair-haired English girl was not to be encouraged. Although she so seldom left her room, she had an uncanny knowledge of all that went on. Selma with unusual tact avoided the subject of her fiancé, and checked her father when he spoke about arrangements for her wedding.

'Oh, discuss all that with Kem,' she told him. 'Ven and I are making the most of our freedom while we're still carefree spinsters. Time enough for all those tiresome details when she's gone.'

It did not seem to occur to him that it was odd she should be so indifferent about her wedding, though it did to Venice. As regards herself, Selma cherished the myth that Venice would become engaged to Bill upon her return, for the idea allayed the few qualms she had felt about appropriating her friend's admirer. She knew that Kem must have been attracted to Venice to so far forget himself as to embrace her, but accustomed to outshining the younger girl, she was certain that she had obliterated any yearnings on Kem's part towards her, but she was not so sure about Venice. Venice played up to her, for the pretence preserved her pride. She would hate Selma to discover that she was in love with Kem.

So for a couple of weeks the girls revelled in the sunshine, sea and sand. The banks of the Bosphorus are crowded with cafés, restaurants and places of entertainment as far as the Black Sea, the villages of Rumelia have merged, or been submerged along the narrow coastal road. But there were other places with wonderful beaches, to be reached by ferry. The Princes Islands in the Sea of Marmara, so called because they were places of exile for members of the imperial Byzantine dynasties, were covered with fir trees, surrounding delightful coves and creeks, with stretches of flat sand. No cars are allowed there except for police jeeps, transport is provided by horses, donkeys or bicycles. Horse buggies can be hired and are called *faytons* from the French *phaeton*. Alternatively the Professor would accompany them for whole days on the European shore of Marmara, taking picnic food with them, for the Turks love picnics and he had acquired the taste for them. Here were villages and small towns built on the sites of ancient civilisations and there was always the chance of finding some interesting remains.

Selma tanned to a glorious tint, almost the colour of copper, and Venice's pale skin acquired an apricot glow. They were timeless days suspended between past and future, and both girls rarely referred to anything that had happened or was to come.

Selma did not seem to miss Kem and seldom spoke of her marriage. He neither wrote nor phoned, but he sent her a parcel by special messenger. It contained a gold and ruby necklace that sent her into ecstasies.

'Now,' she said, trying it on, 'I shall look like a sultana.' It was a barbaric ornament, not new, and might well have adorned the neck of a seraglio favourite. He had already given her a ring, which she seldom wore, saying she was afraid of losing it on the beaches.

Her attitude troubled Venice, who genuinely wanted her friend to be happy. She did not seem like a girl in love, though she periodically declared she was devoted to her fiancé for Venice's benefit, and Venice knew that Kem was not in love with her, and it was on his part a marriage of convenience. But if he did not love Selma, he would come to do so when she bore him a son, as it was to be hoped she would. He was sufficiently Oriental in outlook to regard that as a matter of prime importance. Venice supposed they would be as happy as most couples were, and wrestled with her own rebellious emotions. Aunt Joan had at least taught her to be a stoic. Kemal was as lost to her as if he had died, and she must get on with her own life as best she could, though she would miss the Hadleighs sorely when she was back in London.

Bill wrote again sending her particulars of an opening that might suit her, advising her to apply for it. It was at a school in the north of England, so it would mean a complete break with her old life. She answered Bill's letters and in each one said she would be glad to see him again, which was true; he was one of her few friends. Eventually he too would find a girl to replace her. She sent off the application with a heavy heart. The north of England seemed like a place of exile.

Selma was pleased that she was to live in Ankara; she had feared she might be expected to reside with Zubeyde Hanim, who had the old-fashioned notion that a daughter-in-law should be at her beck and call and take over the duties that she found onerous.

'That joy will be for Ahmet's wife when he gets one,' she told Venice. 'I shall be independent and mistress of my own house.'

Selma had never been to the capital, though she had visited the Mediterranean coast of Anatolia during holidays with her father, so the Professor suggested they should take a trip there for a couple of days and see what it was like. Venice's holiday was drawing to a close and the expedition would be a pleasant end to it, for of course she must go with them. Selma was all for it.

'You'd like to see where I'm going to live, wouldn't you, darling?' she enquired. 'I'm sure you'd enjoy a visit to Anatolia, and I hope you and Bill will come and stay with me when I'm installed there.'

Venice remarked that Bill was allergic to foreign travel, while she wondered what excuse she could make to avoid going to Ankara.

'Then you'll have to persuade him to give it a try,' Selma persisted. 'He may find he likes it.'

Venice agreed he might, concealing the fact that she expected her friendship with Bill to fade, nor could she possibly stay as a guest in Kemal's house when he was married. But that was a matter for the future. Her present problem was how to exclude herself from the proposed expedition without offending the Hadleighs.

She found it would be impossible. If she feigned illness, Selma would feel bound to stay with her, a faked message demanding her immediate return would be impracticable as she was to go home on the day following the Ankara trip. A hint about expenses produced the assurance that she would be the Hadleighs' guest. Added to which she very much wanted to see the Turkish capital, an opportunity that was unlikely to come her way again, and it seemed a little hard that the complication with Kemal should defraud her of it.

Professor Hadleigh proposed to fly there, spend a night at a hotel, look round the town, inspect Kem's house and fly back in time for Venice's flight to England the next morning.

'Due to my unfortunate mishap the beginning of your holiday was spoiled,' he told Venice. 'I'd like this little jaunt to be some sort of recompense for my stupidity.'

'But I got a voyage to Russia which I shouldn't have had but for that,' Venice pointed out, stifling a wave of nostalgia. Yalta ... the Black Sea ... Kemal at the Palace of Livadia ... if the Professor had not wrecked himself so much pain might have been avoided, but she would not have it otherwise. It would be something to look back upon all her life.

'Don't suppose that was much fun for you,' Lucas Hadleigh remarked innocently. 'This time you shall have the best accommodation and revel in luxury. I owe you a debt for being so kind to Selma and me.'

'There, Ven, that's a handsome offer,' Selma declared. 'Why are you looking so dubious? Surely you want to come?'

Venice said she did. After all, Kem would have time only for Selma and surely he could not blame her for coming?

'It'll be very hot,' her host warned her. 'August isn't the ideal month to go there, but it's only for a couple of days. It's pleasantest in spring and autumn, the winters are terribly cold.'

'You won't like that, Sel,' Venice commented, for her friend was a hothouse plant.

'I can always go somewhere else for the winter,' Selma pointed out. 'I'm not going to be stuck there, I hope.'

Her father looked disapproving. 'A wife's place is with her husband,' he told her sternly, and Selma stuck out her tongue at him.

Venice was aware of intense excitement as they boarded the plane, and it was not all due to the prospect of seeing Ankara. Kemal was to meet them at the airport and drive them to their hotel. He had been warned that she would be of the party, and she hoped he would not misinterpret her presence, and she would have a chance to explain her dilemma. Deep down inside her she knew that she was longing to see him once more before she parted from him for ever.

Selma wore the thinnest of white muslin dresses under a linen dust coat. She had wanted to wear trousers, but that her father forbade.

130

'You must remember Kemal's position,' he told her.

'A load of rubbish,' Selma grumbled to Venice. 'I can see Ankara needs me to liven it up.' She was seeing herself as a leader of fashion in the capital.

Venice wore a green outfit that matched her eyes with a shady hat, for she hated sunglasses, and rarely put hers on. Selma had one of the new sun visors, which Venice thought was far from becoming, but it was more often in her hand than on her forehead.

Ankara, formerly Angora, is Ataturk's creation. He changed it from a backward country town to a huge modern city.

All Turkey is haunted by the memory of Mustapha Kemal. His grateful countrymen have put up many monuments in his honour and named countless streets in his name, but it is in Ankara he is revered most deeply. It was his headquarters during the War of Independence and when it was won, tens of thousands of homeless and jobless Turks answered his call to erect new houses, lay out roads and install amenities. It was a revelation of what one man's inspiration can do in a short space of time. Here he planned and imposed the revolutionary reforms that changed the face of his country. Here also he is buried, Kemal the Perfect, Ataturk, the Father of the Turks, the Ghazi, the Conqueror.

His mausoleum crowns a hill opposite to the one on which stands the Hisar, the ancient citadel, which dates back to the Romans. This old fortress holds within its walls a warren of narrow lanes in which the old way of life still persists, for in the modern city of government offices and straight new boulevards there is little to be seen of the colour and charm of old-time Turkey among the throngs of white-collar workers who live and labour there.

To this place redolent of Ataturk with whom she

was apt to identify the man she knew, also called Kemal, Venice was brought on a blazingly hot summer's day.

Kem was waiting for them at the airport. As he came towards them Venice was struck anew by the aura of forceful energy that emanated from him. There were other men at the airport, taller and handsomer, but beside him they faded into insignificance or appeared clumsy. He was dressed in fawn trousers and shirt with a tailored linen jacket. Except for the formality of his attire, he looked as Western as the American and British tourists flowing through, and much more so than the Italians and Spaniards.

He shook the professor's hand warmly, touched Selma's cheek lightly with a finger tip and bowed formally to Venice. The grey eyes met hers unflinchingly, but they were cold as ice. She knew then that he furiously resented her appearance, and she should not have come. He might even imagine that she had deliberately engineered this visit to re-establish contact between them with the hope of weaning him from Selma, a supposition that made her writhe inwardly as she strove to maintain a calm aloofness. This special treat that the Professor had arranged for her was going to be little short of torture. Kem wanted to forget her, to eliminate entirely an episode he regretted, and she had had the effrontery to remind him of her existence. Too late she understood his feelings, but she would have to go through her ordeal with the best grace she could muster. Mercifully it would be of short duration and she would keep in the background as much as possible.

Kem had brought his own car to meet them, and Selma as of right got into the front passenger seat, though he had indicated that the Professor should do so.

'Pa'll sit behind with Ven,' she announced.

Kem raised his brows but made no protest, merely held the rear door open for Venice to enter. She did so with heightened colour, avoiding looking at him. The sight of his lean spruce figure, his thin tanned face, had set her pulses racing, but she could sense no response in him. His strength of will would allow no back-sliding, and the fairy's child had ceased to enchant him.

Kemal made polite enquiries about their journey, answered Selma's coquettish remarks with chilly courtesy, and addressed no single word to Venice. The citadel came into sight on its impressive mount. Below it the modern town spread its boulevards and residences.

'We have everything here,' Kem told Selma. 'Shops, theatres, cinemas, night clubs, museums and of course mosques.'

Selma viewed the prospect with a crease between her brows.

'It's an awful long way from civilisation.'

'What do you mean?' he asked sharply. 'Of course it is civilised. Here are universities, the parliament, embassies and even parks, though they take a great deal of preservation in this dry climate.'

Selma subsided, but the crease remained between her fine eyebrows. Istanbul has become cosmopolitan, but Ankara is Turkish. It is many miles from the sea, and vistas away from Europe. She had never felt isolated in Rumelia, but she did here, and she was filled with dismay.

Rooms had been booked for them in a modern hotel on the Ataturk Bulvari, which was one of the best parts of the town. Kemal said that they would need to rest after their journey in the heat and he would call in the evening to take them out to dinner.

'In the morning we will look at the house before you go back, if you are agreeable,' he suggested.

Lucas Hadleigh said those arrangements would be perfect, but he was not going to rest, but visit the Hittite museum.

'You should come too, Selma,' he told her. 'It's unique, and you ought to learn something about the early history of your country to be.'

'It'll keep,' she returned sullenly. 'It's much too hot to go sightseeing. You go, Ven'll stop with me—won't you, darling?'

There was an almost desperate appeal in her dark eyes.

Venice said she would, though she would have liked to see something of the town in spite of the heat. Kem offered to give the Professor a lift as it was some way to the museum, and so they parted.

The girls were sharing a room and as soon as they were installed, Selma began to pace it with quick nervous steps.

'I don't like it here,' she burst out. 'I can't think why Kem won't live in Istanbul.'

'It seems a very fine city to me,' Venice told her soothingly. 'And Kem's work is here. It only seems a little strange at first, you'll soon get used to it. Besides, you'll ...' she swallowed painfully, 'you'll be living with the man you love, that should compensate for everything.'

'Oh, you're always so sentimental,' Selma exclaimed. She gave her friend a sly look. 'But of course I do love Kem,' she declared with emphasis, 'and he's of some importance here. Couldn't you come and live with us, Ven, until I've got used to it?'

'Good God, no!' Venice cried, appalled by this suggestion.

'Of course I was forgetting Bill, he's more to you than me,' Selma said resentfully.

'He's nothing to do with it,' Venice declared, 'but

such an arrangement simply would not work, Sel. Kem wouldn't like it for a start, and married people should be on their own. Look, darling, you're tired, the dust and heat have been too much for you. Have a little sleep and you'll feel much better.'

She helped Selma to undress and shower—the room was connected to a bathroom with adequate plumbing, she found with relief—assisted her into a wrap, and on to the bed. Within a few moments Selma was sound asleep. Venice stood looking down at the beautiful petulant face framed in black hair strewing the pillow and wondered if Kem realised what he was taking on. Selma was spoilt and was used to her own way. If she decided against Ankara and he refused to move she could make his life a hell. Venice sighed and turned away to take her own shower. She would soon be far away and could do nothing to help. They would have to work out their own destiny as best they could.

Selma that evening was a different person. She decked herself in a flaming red dress that clung to her figure provocatively, and left her arms and shoulders bare, subduing it slightly but hardly enough with a black open-knit shawl. Her cheeks were brilliant with colour and her great eyes sparkling. About her neck blazed the gold and ruby collar Kem had given her.

They went to a restaurant in the same street, the Kebapei Bursa, where Kem said they could obtain a real Turkish dish, the Bursa Kebab, which turned out to be a mixed grill served on flat unleavened bread and garnished with grilled tomatoes and green peppers, the whole topped with yogurt.

Kem seemed unable to take his eyes off Selma throughout the meal, but Venice, watching, sensed that his regard was not wholly admiring, until she decided her doubt was prompted by jealousy. Naturally he was enthralled by so much beauty and brilliance, even if Selma were a little overdressed. She herself was wearing a simple jersey dress in a subdued pattern of mauves, pinks and blue, sweet pea colours, with long sleeves and a demure neckline. She had put colour on her cheeks to disguise their pallor, which had shown even under her suntan, for the heat and suppressed emotion had drained her. Her bleached hair shone silver in the subdued lighting of the restaurant, the ghost of a girl, but for her eyes, which were jade green and bright with unshed tears. She was there on sufferance at Selma's request and she tried to make herself as inconspicuous as possible. That was not difficult, for Selma monopolised the conversation, teasing Kem and her father, exclaiming over the food and the decor of the restaurant, also making it was to be hoped inaudible comments upon the other diners which were more witty than flattering. Many of them kept glancing in her direction, the ladies with condemnation, their accompanying males with open admiration.

Kemal was cool, courteous and aloof under her badinage. He never looked at Venice. The white dinner jacket he had put on in Selma's honour became him and he was immaculately groomed, but his face was inscrutable, the grey eyes unfathomable as they rested upon his fiancée.

At one time during the meal Venice noticed a sinister-looking character at a distant table who seemed to be watching them with concentration. She drew the Professor's attention to him, who in turn spoke to Kemal.

'He doesn't seem to like you. Have you any enemies, Kem?'

Kemal threw the man an indifferent glance.

'I know the fellow,' he told them. 'He is one of the *agas*, the big landowners, of which there are still far too many. I support the agrarian policies Ataturk died before he could implement, that all the land should belong to the peasants, so he would like to see me eliminated.'

'You mean you're in danger?' Selma gasped.

He shrugged his shoulders. 'No more than any other politician. It is a profession that has its occupational risks like any other.'

Having finished his meal, the man stood up and Venice half expected he would come to speak to them, and hoped he would not cause a brawl, but after giving Kem a venomous glance he went out.

It was much cooler when they went outside. Ankara stands so high that the evenings turn chilly. They went to the car and debated what to do next. The mausoleum complex and the citadel were both floodlit and Selma said:

'Why not visit your hero's shrine, Kem? I'm sure you'd like to take me there.'

'No!' he exclaimed so violently that they were astonished. He added quietly: 'You are not suitably dressed.'

'I suppose I should wear black and a crêpe veil,' she said insolently.

'It would be more seemly,' he returned, unperturbed by her intended provocation.

In the end they decided to go to a night club where they could dance with the tourists which Ankara was beginning to attract. When they had arrived, Venice lingered after getting out of the car, while Selma and the Professor were looking at a poster advertising a belly dancer. Kem was locking the car. She said to him in a low pleading voice:

'Kem, I'm sorry about this. If I could have got out of coming I would have done, but it wasn't possible.'

He straightened himself and his grey glance flickered over her, before he looked away.

'You have no need to apologise, Venice Hanim; it was an opportunity you could hardly miss.' Was there a double meaning behind his cold voice? 'I trust you will enjoy your brief sojourn in our capital.'

He spoke like a polite stranger, denying there had ever been anything between them. Then Selma called to her and she went to join her. Once inside, Selma monopolised Kem, who it transpired was proficient in Western dancing. Venice sat with the Professor, who entertained her by describing the exhibits in the Hittite museum. Presently he became aware that this was not a very entertaining subject for a young girl.

'You should be dancing,' he exclaimed. 'Selma mustn't be selfish. Kem can spare you a dance, I'm sure, or find you a partner. He must know people here.'

He half rose from his seat, but Venice pulled him down again.

'Please, no. I don't want to dance. I'm rather tired and I'm quite happy watching.'

He chuckled. 'Some of the contortions of the youngsters here are quite an exhibition.' He subsided, though only half convinced.

A floor show by Turkish belly-dancers drove the amateurs to their seats, but Kemal and Selma sat at a distance from them. Venice tried not to feel hurt by Kem's neglect. She would have liked to have told him that she was leaving for England on the day after the morrow and say goodbye, but such lingerings were, she supposed, a feminine weakness. He had ruthlessly cut her out of his life and desired no further contact with her.

They left after the dancers' act and at their hotel, Kemal arranged to pick up the Hadleighs in the morning. Venice excused herself, feeling she would be intruding on a family matter. Selma only protested faintly and Kemal looked relieved, while the Professor said:

'It will hardly interest you, my dear, you'd better take the chance of exploring the town.'

'You must not wander about alone,' Kemal said curtly. It was the first time he had voluntarily addressed her.

'Nonsense,' Lucas Hadleigh objected. 'Your countrymen consider her to be a guest and no one would insult her.'

'There are not only Turks about,' Kemal reminded him, but he made no further demur. He came in with them and Venice said goodnight to him in the lounge. He returned her courtesy stiffly, avoiding her eyes. She did not notice as she sadly made her exit that his hands were clenched.

The two girls had breakfast in their room and Venice waited upstairs until Selma and her father had gone. She meant to visit the mausoleum. She had heard so much about Ataturk it seemed the thing to do in this his city, also it was a link with Kemal, who had educated her about the founder of the republic. She was sure that he often went there himself and something of his presence might linger there. Though she scolded herself for her sentimentality, which Selma had derided, she set forth in better spirits than she had been in since her arrival.

She went up the marble Lions' Walk, attaching herself to a party of tourists bent upon the same errand. On each side were pavilions with bas-relief carvings. At the far end was a square surrounded by a colonnade, all the buildings being modern in style. In the middle of the square a high mast bore the red Turkish flag with its star and crescent. Sailors in white and soldiers in olive green uniforms stood on guard. From thence a huge staircase led up to the golden-coloured mausoleum. Venice found herself in an immense high hall with gold mosaics between seven tall windows. It held a solitary marble sarcophagus, which she knew was symbolic, for the Ghazi's remains were in the vault below.

She remained for a long while by the impressive tomb thinking of all she had read and been told about that most remarkable man, who was so reverenced by the one she loved. Characters like Ataturk are only born once in a hundred years, but if Kemal Osman had been alive then she was sure he would have distinguished himself. He possessed the same ruthless singleness of purpose that his leader had. Such men leave their mark on history.

At length she turned away. Her Turkish holiday was over and it was fitting that she should pay homage to Turkey's saviour on this her last day. After lunch they would be going to the airport and back to Istanbul and her last night on Turkish soil. She steeled herself to show sympathetic interest in Selma's rhapsodies about her new home. It was the last service she would perform for her.

CHAPTER EIGHT

To Venice's surprise and dismay she found that Kemal was to accompany them back to Istanbul. Every moment in the presence of this cold stranger was purgatory to her. In the aircraft he sat with Selma across the aisle from herself and the Professor, who gallantly insisted that Venice must have the window seat. She tried to concentrate on the scene below her, miles of arid landscape crossed by hills, but she could not help noticing that Selma was being unusually quiet. Occasionally she gave Kem a reproachful glance and Venice wondered what had happened to quench her normal high spirits. She had expected she would be full of chatter about her new home, possibly she was feeling the heat.

Kemal drove them back to the Villa Yasmin in a hired car, which he had arranged to meet them at the airport. He told the Professor that he would call for Venice in the early morning to take her to catch her flight, so he need not bother to make any arrangements about transport for her. Selma instantly said she would get up early and come with her to see her off.

'You don't mind, Kem?' she asked.

'Of course not. I expected you would want to come.'

Venice wondered what he would have done if Selma had decided otherwise, for he would not have wanted to be alone with her, but it transpired he had previously mentioned it to Selma, and they made the final arrangements without consulting her, as if in fact she was not there. She wanted to tell them not to trouble, that she would take herself to the airport, but she knew there would be difficulties and Selma would be put out, so she decided to let the matter rest. Afterwards she was to be thankful she had not asserted her independence.

Upon arrival at the house, Kemal took Selma to pay her respects to Zubeyde Hanim, who would like to hear what she thought of Ankara; the Professor was tired with all his exertions and went to rest. Venice occupied herself with packing, leaving out only what she would need for the night, and the clothes she would wear for the journey. She had informed her aunt that she would be back on the date she mentioned, and was not looking forward to her acid comments upon what she considered to be an extravagant and un- necessary holiday abroad, but she would be glad to see Bill again. His at least was a friendly face, and per- haps she would discover that he meant something to her after all, though she thought that was unlikely.

Venice had gone to bed when Selma came home, wanting to have a good night before her early start. She felt so drained and weary she was sure she would sleep. She had already dropped off when Selma came into her room wearing one of her extravagant neg- ligées. Venice awoke with a start and gazed at her dazedly.

'Sorry to disturb you, Ven,' Selma said perfunctorily, 'but I must talk to you or I'll bust. It's no use saying anything to Pa, he wouldn't understand. Ven, I don't know what to do.'

As so often in the past she perched herself on the foot of Venice's bed. Her hair hung over her shoulders in a black cloud and her great eyes were tragic.

'Has something gone wrong?' Venice asked sleepily. She did not feel receptive to Selma's confidences. She had probably had a tiff with Kem and had blown it up into a major tragedy.

'That house—it was awful!' Selma declared. 'I

wouldn't have minded one of those modern ones, they didn't look too bad, but it's an old Ottoman house, partly built of wood, and though plumbing has been installed it's not up to date, and sometimes the water doesn't run properly. Kem seemed to think it was a joke, but I didn't find it at all funny. It's up by that grim old castle where those narrow streets are, and they're so insanitary. I can't live there, Ven.'

'I suppose Kem could find you something better,' Venice suggested, wishing Selma would go. Her domestic problems were nothing to do with her.

'Not him, he thinks it's marvellous,' Selma said despairingly. 'And that's not all. You know I never took the idea of teaching seriously. Pa insisted I should train for something and I wanted to be with you, but I never expected I'd ever have to do it.'

She paused and twisted her hands together.

'Well, you won't, will you?' said Venice.

'That's what I thought, but I find Kem expects me to use my training,' Selma wailed. 'He's got a job lined up for me to teach English at the university in Ankara. It seems his precious Ataturk wanted women to work alongside their men. He talks a lot of hot air about the importance of education and seems to consider I've got a mission to teach young Turks about Western ways. Could anything be more gruesome?'

Venice felt some of Selma's dismay. Did Kemal understand Selma so little that he imagined she would consent to such a proposition? She raised herself on her pillows and sought for arguments to placate her.

'Darling, you know Kem is a dedicated man,' she said gently. 'Can't you humour him for a while? When you have children he won't expect you to go on working, and after all, you worked for your diplomas. It seems a pity to waste them.'

'If I'd had any sense I'd have failed my exams,' Selma

declared regretfully, 'instead of letting you push me through them. I don't want that sort of life, Ven, I want plenty of fun and amusement while I'm young, and a husband who'll play with me, not a pillar of the state.'

'Then perhaps you'd better not marry him,' Venice suggested a little tartly. It seemed a little ironic that she had been called upon to plead Kem's cause with Selma. She herself would not have minded an old house and would deem it a privilege to be able to assist him with his reformatory ideas, but she had not been given Selma's opportunity.

It was the wrong thing to have said. Selma immediately flared up, she must marry Kemal, there was no one she liked better, but if he loved her surely he could be persuaded to live somewhere else and make her wishes of prime importance?

Venice was fairly certain that Kem did not love Selma and it was unlikely he would indulge her whims. His position required him to live in Anatolia and the house had family associations for him, but he might let her off the teaching if she expressed her repugnance.

'Have you discussed it with Zubeyde Hanim?' Venice asked, for Selma had spent most of the evening with her.

Selma smiled. 'One doesn't discuss things with Zubeyde,' she said. 'She lays down the law. She's thankful to get me out of the way before I corrupt her precious Ahmet, and she's only too pleased I've chosen Kem. He hasn't mentioned the teaching idea to her and he's asked me not to, since her ideas are reactionary. She'd sooner see me in purdah, but when he told me it about put the lid on.'

'You haven't had time to think things through,' Venice told her. 'At least Kem is modern in his outlook. Perhaps the house could be altered to suit you, and there's plenty going on in Ankara.'

Selma pleated the counterpane. 'It's such a dead end,' she complained. 'Right in the middle of nowhere—I'll be cut off from everyone.'

'With a daily air service to Istanbul?' Venice queried. Selma merely looked mutinous, and she went on. 'But you love Kem, don't you? That should compensate for a few inconveniences.'

Selma flashed her a jealous look.

'Of course you think that—where thou goest I will go, and all that mush. But it *is* me Kem wants to marry, and he's quite something, so dynamic. If only he thought more of me and less of his beastly politics I'd be happy.'

'You can't separate a man from his life's work,' Venice told her sagely. 'Love isn't as absorbing to a man as to a woman.'

Selma thumped the bedclothes, narrowly missing Venice's feet.

'That's just it. I want him to be madly and passionately in love with me to the exclusion of anything else, and he isn't!'

Venice sighed. Selma was more perceptive than she had thought, but what could she say to console her?

'But as you've said, he *has* asked you to marry him,' she said patiently, 'And I suppose he had plenty of others to choose from. It's up to you to make yourself indispensable to him.'

'Is that what you'd do?' Selma asked.

'Of course, a good wife should.'

'Sounds so unromantic,' Selma pouted, and Venice realised what a child she still was, and a spoilt child at that.

She gave Venice a long considering look, and Venice had an uneasy suspicion that she had accepted Kem more because she resented his attachment to herself than because she really cared about him. When she had said that she had no use for love eternal she had spoken the truth and all Kem represented to her was sexual excitement, and triumph over a rival. Hitherto there had never been any conflict between them; Selma despised Bill and Venice had never come between her and any of her swains. That Venice could win from Kem the response she wanted for herself was a sufficient spur to urge her to take possession of him.

'I don't know what to do,' Selma said. 'I won't give him up, and I don't suppose he would let me, but I don't want to live his life.'

'Have another talk with Kem,' Venice advised. 'Tell him you'd rather be a housewife than a teacher so you can devote all your time to him. He's Turk enough to appreciate that.' She smiled wanly. 'Visit Ankara again, it may improve when you know it better.'

'But it's terrible in the winter,' Selma declared, 'so cold.' She looked at Venice coaxingly. 'Couldn't you talk to Kem? You could put my point of view much better than I can.'

'Certainly not!' Venice exclaimed, horrified. At Selma's hurt expression, she went on more gently, 'No, darling, I couldn't interfere, this is between you and him. Besides, I'm going home tomorrow and I shan't have the opportunity.'

'Don't go,' Selma pleaded. 'I'll be lost without you.'

'That's absurd.' Venice's patience was nearly at an end. 'You've got your father and Zubeyde Hanim, to say nothing of poor Kemal . . .'

'Poor Kemal!' Selma interrupted. 'Of course your sympathies are all with him. What a pity you're not me, you'd suit him much better.'

Venice winced and turned her head sideways. This was hitting below the belt. Not only was she not Selma,

146

but she was English and had no rich dowry to add to her attractions. Luckily Selma had not got round to realising that her endowment might be an inducement, or perhaps she accepted that as a matter of course. Money had never been important to Selma because she had always had plenty of it.

Selma glanced maliciously at her averted face, and then her expression softened.

'I shouldn't have said that,' she admitted. 'It conjured up too many might-have-beens, didn't it? But you've got your Bill.'

'Yes, I've got Bill,' Venice agreed mendaciously.

'But he isn't a patch on Kem.'

'Naturally you think so, that's as it should be,' Venice said firmly. She straightened herself in the bed, and smoothed her pillows. 'Now you've got that load off your chest, you should feel better, and if you don't mind, I'd like to get to sleep. I have to be up early in the morning, and so will you if you're coming to see me off.'

'Of course I'm coming, but it's so unnecessary,' Selma declared. 'Why can't you stay with me indefinitely?'

'I certainly couldn't, I've got to find myself a job.'

'Couldn't you get one in Turkey? I'm sure Kem could find you one, and Bill too for that matter. No one can teach English better than a native.'

'Thank you, but no. Be sensible, Sel, you're clinging to me now because you've got cold feet about your future, but once you're married you'll have no further use for me.'

'I'll always want you,' Selma declared fervently.

'Unless you start to get jealous again.' Venice wanted to put an end to Selma's persuasions which were a little painful. She would like very much to remain in Turkey, but to let Selma consult Kemal about work for her was unthinkable.

Selma stood up, drawing her wrap about her rounded figure.

'I'd have no cause,' she declared cruelly. 'Kem's fancy for you is over, that I do know.'

Venice felt the stab. Kemal's attitude in Ankara towards her provided the proof of that. Selma's dark eyes were again malicious.

'You've given me plenty of advice, let me give you some. When you get back to Bill, don't mention Kem to him. He mightn't believe there'd been nothing between you. Goodnight.'

She went out of the room, but she had banished all desire for sleep from Venice. Selma, half child, half woman, was swayed by conflicting emotions and desires. Kem's magnetic personality had fired her imagination as it had Venice's own, but she was not interested in the man himself. She wanted a romantic lover ready to obey her slightest wish, which Kem would never do. Venice could see little chance of real happiness for either of them, except that, Selma being pliable, Kem's stronger character might be able to mould her into the role he planned for her to play. Eventually Selma might submit to being the subservient wife, conditioned by her oriental blood inherited from generations of women who had been subject to male dominance. Kemal, for all his Western ideas, could, she was sure, be an effective domestic tyrant. It was not Venice's idea of a happy union, but it might possibly work out.

In the morning Venice rose unrested and completed her packing. She drank the coffee the maid brought to her room, refusing anything to eat. The Professor was not dressed, and met her at the doorway of his room in his dressing gown, to say goodbye. She noticed he was beginning to look rather frail and was glad he would have Kem's strength and efficiency to lean upon in the running of his varied interests. He thanked her for her goodness to Selma and she thanked him for all his generosity to her.

'You must come out for her wedding,' he told her, and she said she hoped to do so, knowing very well she would not.

Selma greeted her with a slightly defiant air, and Venice guessed she was regretting her confidences of the night before. She looked beautiful in a flowered two-piece, a skirt, not trousers; already she was deferring to Kemal's wishes. Venice wore her green travelling outfit, but there was no sparkle in her eyes, and she looked wan with dark smudges under them.

Kem brought the car to the door, and got out of it with his usual agility. He gave her a formal 'Good morning,' without looking at her. She settled herself in the rear seat while he was putting her cases in the boot. Selma took her place in front, and he slid in beside her. The car moved off, while the two domestics waved from the terrace, with their usual friendliness.

'*Güle-güle*,' they called.

Venice knew it meant literally laughing-laughing, being interpreted as 'Go with a smile.' She would try to do that; the last Kem should see of her would be a smiling face.

Mist hung over the Bosphorus, dispersing slowly in the rays of the rising sun. The domes and minarets of Istanbul were dark silhouettes against the brightening sky. In another twenty-four hours, Venice thought, the city and its surroundings would have become only a memory to be recalled when she was feeling reminiscent. Kemal's smooth head set upon his strong shoulders was all she could see of him. Soon he too would be nothing but a shadow from the past.

Airport reception was full of bustle and crowded with people. Kemal put her cases upon the weighing machine as she went to the counter to show her ticket. Selma was looking woebegone as she realised this was a final parting with Venice. Throughout all the vicissitudes their relationship had undergone, she still retained her old affection for her friend, but Venice did not deceive herself that it would long survive their parting.

As she moved away from the counter, Venice found herself standing next to Kemal. She never knew what it was that made her look towards the crowd near the entrance; some sixth sense had conveyed a warning. There was a gap between them and the first of the surging passengers, on the fringe of which she saw the man they had noticed in the restaurant at Ankara, and even as she recognised him, he raised his right hand. She knew with a sickening certainty what it held. With an inarticulate cry she sprang forward, pushing Kemal aside; she felt something hit her shoulder and knew no more.

It was some time before Venice discovered that she was in the American Hospital at Nisantasi. For several days she had been hovering between life and death. The bullet that had been aimed for Kemal's heart had passed through her shoulder, entering under the clavicle and bruising her shoulder-blade on its way out. It was a clean wound, but she had contracted a fever. Of what had happened at the airport after she was hit she had a few vague recollections of shouting and confusion as she began to come round, after her arm had been given first aid, searing pain and a sedative being administered, and Kem's voice, thick with emotion:

'You said you would die for me, and you nearly have.'

Then oblivion when presumably she was loaded into the ambulance that had been sent for. During those first days she was kept mostly under sedation, and her waking moments were filled with hallucinations. She recognised Professor Hadleigh, but muttered that he should be in Russia. Selma too, and her beautiful face floated before Venice's fevered vision.

'Why aren't you with your husband in Ankara?' she demanded fretfully, though her words were indistinguishable. Selma vanished with a stricken look.

'She doesn't love him,' Venice whispered. 'Oh, Kem ... Kem!' But Kemal did not come, nor did Selma come again. She hated illness and her brief visit was only a painful duty. She was horrified by her friend's appearance, her flushed face, wandering eyes, and her hair cropped short. She had fled precipitately and not all her father's persuasions could get her to repeat her visit.

Eventually Venice's temperature went down, the wound began to heal and she awoke one morning to full consciousness. She gazed in bewilderment around the white antiseptic room in which she found herself, and noticed it was filled with flowers, while she tried to recall all that had occurred. Then she became aware that someone was sitting beside her, and thought she must be still feverish, for the gaunt figure in rusty black was her aunt Joan.

'You aren't real, are you?' she asked in a weak thread of a voice.

'Of course I'm real,' Joan Franklin said tartly, 'though I don't wonder you're surprised to see me in this outlandish place—all those heathen temples.' She smiled grimly. 'A right mess you've landed yourself in with your foreign travel! I always said going abroad wasn't safe, but thank God you've recovered your senses.'

'And you've come all this way to see me?' Venice was immensely touched.

'I was notified of the accident as your next of kin and that you were at death's door,' Aunt Joan said stiffly. 'I considered it my duty to come and see that you were buried properly with Christian rites. After all, you're my only relation and Derek's daughter.'

Her hard face softened momentarily and she laid her hand over Venice's thin one lying on the coverlet. Venice was too weak to grasp it, but she felt that a miracle had occurred. In spite of the macabre reason given for her journey her aunt was betraying that she had some affection for her.

Then a nurse appeared and told the visitor she would have to leave.

'Miss Franklin isn't strong enough to talk,' she said. 'You can come again tomorrow.'

Aunt Joan rose to her feet, a meagre black figure, and to Venice's amazement kissed her brow.

'Get well quickly,' she said gruffly, and followed the nurse out of the room. What nationality the latter was, Venice had no idea, but she did not think she was Turkish.

From that point on Venice began to regain strength rapidly. She had youth and a good constitution on her side. On her aunt's next visit she was sitting up in bed supported by a back rest and pillows. Joan Franklin told her that Professor Hadleigh had found her accommodation near the hospital and was being more than kind.

'Seems to think he's indebted to you, though I should say the boot's on the other foot,' she said. 'Wasn't his fault you got shot at the airport. Nasty dangerous places they are, always having incidents, as they call them, with innocent people getting what wasn't meant for them. I never thought my niece would get mixed up in a *News of the World* story.'

'Was it reported in the *News of the World*?' Venice

asked anxiously, having no wish for notoriety.

'Well, no, but it ought to have been,' Aunt Joan said with obvious disappointment.

Venice hesitated. She longed to ask if Kem was all right, but her aunt probably would not know who he was, nor did she seem to suspect that Venice had deliberately intercepted the bullet intended for him. Possibly nobody did realise that, which was the way she wanted it. She wondered if the Hadleighs had sent the flowers. Professor Hadleigh must be so relieved that his future son-in-law had escaped, he felt bound to show his gratitude to the unlucky victim of the 'accident', or didn't he know the shot had been meant for Kem? She hoped he would come and see her soon and tell her what had happened.

As soon as she was considered strong enough she was interviewed by a police officer. A dapper little man, he came to obtain a statement from her. He told her that the assassin had crashed in his car as he tried to make his getaway and had been conveniently killed, so there would be no trial.

'It is believed he intended to shoot Kemal Osman Bey,' he told her, 'with whom he was on bad terms. Turkey owes you a debt for being in the way.' He chuckled as if he considered that it was a joke. 'He is a man we could ill afford to lose.'

He looked at her curiously. Everyone knew Kemal Osman was betrothed to Selma Hadleigh, but it would be so much more romantic if she had been the one to suffer, instead of a stranger, as he believed Venice to be.

'It is a pity he got a foreigner,' he observed. 'I am afraid it will give you a bad impression of Turkey. Believe me, such incidents are no more common here than anywhere else.'

'I don't blame your country,' Venice assured him. 'It

was just an unfortunate accident.'

'Once you have signed your statement, you will be free to go,' he told her pompously. 'But please to leave us your home address.'

Venice was startled; she had never dreamed she could be detained.

The policeman asked her a few questions about the dead man. Had she ever seen him before? She said not, for after all she could not be sure that he was the same person as the character she had noticed in the restaurant in Ankara, and she wanted to be involved as little as possible.

'We know his identity, of course,' the policeman said, 'but we would like to discover if he had accomplices.'

Venice felt a thrill of fear.

'Then Kemal Bey may be in further danger?' she asked faintly.

He shrugged his shoulders beneath his neat uniform.

'Not necessarily. We live in a violent age, *hanim*, but be assured we will do our best to protect Osman Bey.'

Venice's statement was short. She merely said that she had been accompanied by Miss Hadleigh and Mr Osman who had come to see her off, when she had suddenly been struck down as she was preparing to enter the departure lounge. Which was perfectly true. There was no need to mention that she had caught sight of a person she thought she had seen before and her inner conviction that he meant to do Kemal harm. The man was dead and the police had identified him. She was not withholding information that could help them.

The day after the policeman's visit, Professor Hadleigh came. He was insistent that Venice should come to recuperate at the Villa Yasmin, but Joan Franklin was anxious to return as soon as she was fit to travel. Venice had no wish to linger longer in Rumelia, so she thanked the Professor very much for his kind offer, but said she felt she really must go home, as there would be matters to attend to. She had given the northern school her home address, thinking she would be back, and there might be an answer.

'But you're still in bed,' he protested.

'I sit up for part of the day, but it seems to be an unwritten law that we receive our visitors in bed,' she said, smiling.

He looked with dissatisfaction at her white face whence all the tan had faded, and her almost transparent hands.

'Well, you must go if you're so determined,' he said. 'I will make the arrangements, to spare your aunt, who is not very good with foreigners.'

They both laughed, knowing Miss Franklin's forthright remarks made her unpopular with those who sought to serve her.

'I shall miss you,' he went on. 'You seem almost like another daughter.'

Tears sprang to Venice's eyes. She cried far too easily now, and this indication of his affection for her moved her.

'I'll miss you too, terribly,' she said shakily. 'I spent many happy hours at your London flat, and I'll never forget all your kindnesses to me.'

'Such a forlorn little waif you were when I first knew you,' he told her reminiscently. 'But you were very good for Selma. A steady friend was what she needed. She's been very tiresome lately—pre-wedding nerves, I suppose. I shall be thankful when she's married, and Kemal won't stand any nonsense. He'll be a lot stricter than I've ever been.'

'I don't see he can do much if she defies him.'

155

The Professor smiled a little grimly. 'This is Turkey,' he observed ominously.

Venice wondered what he expected Kem to do—shut Selma up or beat her if she were insubordinate? Not a happy prospect on the eve of her marriage. The Professor moved uncomfortably.

'I'm sorry she hasn't been to see you,' he said apologetically. 'She did come once when you were at your worst and your appearance gave her such a shock she wouldn't come again. She ... shrinks from illness, but now you're yourself again she'll be along.'

So Selma's face had not been an image created by her fevered brain. She hesitated, wanting to ask if Kem had been, but thought better of it. Kem had no reason to suppose that her 'accident' had been anything but a faulty aim on the part of the assassin. He would not feel that he owed her anything and preferred to keep out of her way, though, she thought wistfully, since he had once been involved with her he might have given some sign. As for the words she thought he had spoken at the airport, they only existed in her imagination.

'I'll be glad to see her,' she said, 'and thank you for all the lovely flowers.'

'Flowers?' The Professor looked round the room. 'They are beautiful, aren't they, but I'm afraid I didn't think of sending any. It must have been Selma.'

Fresh ones arrived every morning, a daily delivery from the florist, a nurse had told her. Selma must have given the order to salve her conscience for her neglect.

Venice was soon sitting up for most of the day and the next time her aunt called she found her on the balcony that ran round the building on to which her room opened. She had been lent a wrap, a white towelling affair, and with Selma's promised visit in mind she asked Joan to buy her something a little more glamorous.

'Waste of money,' the elder woman declared. 'There's nothing wrong with what you've got on, though it does look like a bath-towel. It's decent, and that's all that matters. What do you want to look glamorous for? You can't after what they've done to your hair.'

Venice ran her hand over her head, realising she had not looked at herself in a mirror since her illness, leaving her toilet entirely in the nurses' hands.

'It doesn't matter,' she said quickly. 'Except that I prefer to have my own things. There was a dressing gown in my luggage.'

'That's still packed,' her aunt told her. 'I went out to fetch it with the Professor so it would be all ready for our departure. He took me to see Mrs Osman next door. His house is fancy enough, but hers is like a pantomime scene for *Aladdin*.'

Venice was amused and wondered what had induced Lucas Hadleigh to effect a meeting between two such incongruous women. It turned out that Zubeyde had been enquiring about her progress and hearing that Miss Franklin was coming to the Villa Yasmin had demanded to see her.

'She seemed a sensible woman for a Turk,' Aunt Joan conceded. 'Though her clothes are a bit weird.'

It transpired that the pair of them had enjoyed themselves deploring the atrocious manners of the rising generation. Joan made no concessions to fashion or to the weather and must have looked quaint in her long coat, flat shoes and black straw hat among Zubeyde's oriental splendour. Venice was touched that Zubeyde had enquired about her.

When her aunt had gone, Venice asked for a hand mirror. She hardly recognised her own face, it had become so thin, and her eyes looked like those of a hungry cat. Her shorn hair was flattened to her scalp, and she tried to fluff it out with a comb, deciding it looked more like a chicken's down than anything else. She laid the mirror down, wondering whatever the Professor had thought of her. She should have made an effort to make herself look more presentable, overcoming the lethargy that incapacitated her.

Not that she could have done much; she did not suppose the hospital would supply her with make-up, and her hair was a hopeless proposition. She was glad then that Kemal had not come. He would have been unable to recognise his fairy's child. Did he ever remember that, she wondered, or was it firmly banished from his mind now he had decided to marry Selma? She was glad that his last sight of her would not be that of the scarecrow she had now become.

CHAPTER NINE

THE next day was dull and raining, so Venice could not go outside. She was taking more notice of her surroundings and realised that she had been privileged to be allotted a private room of her own. The Hadleigh munificence again, she supposed, though about that she was wrong, as she was to discover at a later date. She resolved that she would contrive to pay the bill herself if she possibly could. She was sitting by the window gazing out at the grey sky and thinking it was the first time she had seen one since her holiday began. Aunt Joan had dropped in for a few moments and announced that she was on her way to buy souvenirs.

'For we'll soon be off now, I hope, and I want something to show my friends that I've really been here,' she declared.

Venice wished she had asked her aunt to bring her back something to read if she could find an English book or papers. She was wrapped in the same white towelling garment she deplored and looked wraith-like except for what she had described to herself, after another glance in the mirror, as her dandelion locks.

The door flew open and Selma burst in, glowing with health and exuberance and followed by, to Venice's acute discomfort, Kem. She caught his shocked expression as he beheld her, and her heart sank. Whatever pretence she had had to good looks had vanished since the incident at the airport.

He remained standing by the door, appearing ill at ease, but Selma ran to her and knelt beside her chair.

'Oh, my poor darling, what have they done to you? You look awful!'

Not a very reassuring observation, Venice thought wryly, with Kemal's attitude confirming it.

'I'm much better than I was,' she told Selma. 'And this'—she touched her head—'will soon grow again. I'm so pleased to see you, darling.'

Selma looked up at her contritely. 'I made a bit of a scene when I first saw you, I was so upset, so they wouldn't let me come again until you were better,' she excused herself.

Venice knew this explanation of her absence was not the entire truth, but she accepted it. One could not expect a butterfly like Selma to hover over sickbeds.

'Weren't you an idiot to get in front of that fellow's gun?' Selma went on. 'It was ill luck, I suppose, that out of all that crowd he managed to wing you. I'll never forget how I felt when you keeled over and I saw you lying there with blood on you.' She shivered violently. 'I wondered who was going to be shot next!'

'Don't think about it,' Venice urged her soothingly, slipping back into her old role of mentor and comforter. 'It's all over now and I'll soon be as good as new.'

She was painfully aware of Kem's aloof figure in the background. Was he never going to speak to her? Then he did, but it was Selma he addressed.

'It was not exactly a revolution, Selma, and I was the person he was aiming at. If it had not been for Venice Hanim's idiocy, as you term it, I should not be here.'

Venice met his eyes over Selma's dark head. They were fixed upon her with a strange expression, almost a kind of awe, a stupid word but the only one that seemed to describe it. Then it flashed into her mind, with the intuition that had always been between them, that he knew it was no accident, and she had deliberately tried to intercept the shot. He had really spoken the words that she had thought she heard when she was half-conscious.

Selma moved her head impatiently. 'Don't exaggerate, Kem dear. He was sure to have missed you. But as Ven says, we won't talk about it any more.'

She stood up, smoothing down the folds of the printed silk dress she was wearing. It was in shades of purple and crimson; it suited her rich opulent beauty and beside her Venice looked like a frail ghost.

'I hear that awful aunt has turned up and wants to drag you back to London,' she went on. 'You mustn't let her, Ven, you must come and spend a long convalescence at the Villa Yasmin. I insist.'

'I'm afraid I can't, dear,' Venice told her quietly. 'Aunt Joan has been surprisingly kind, and it was very noble of her to come out here to see me. It's high time I set about looking for work.'

'But you're not fit.'

'I soon shall be. It's only having my hair cropped that makes me look ... so awful.'

She was aware that Kem made an involuntary movement of protest, but he said nothing.

Selma looked round the room.

'These must be our flowers,' she said. 'We ordered them to be sent every day.'

'How sweet of you, but your father knew nothing about them.'

'No more he did. By our I meant Kem and me. Actually he gave the order,' Selma said carelessly.

'It was the least we could do,' Kemal supported her.

Venice suspected that he had prompted Selma, who would not have thought of them herself. She gave him a swift look of gratitude, then turned her head away, trying to suppress the trembling of her lips. He was looking embarrassed and she was sure he was wishing he had not come.

'It was the very least we could do,' he repeated.

Selma suddenly clapped her hand to her mouth in consternation.

'The fruit!' she exclaimed, 'and the paperbacks. We've left them in the car. Give me the keys, Kem, and I'll get them.'

'If you will allow me . . .'

'No, I'll go. I got some books for Pa too and you won't know which is which. The keys, please.'

He handed them to her and she sped away calling: 'I'll be back in a sec!' leaving the impression that she was glad of an excuse to leave the room.

Left alone with Venice, Kem came over to the window. He stood beside her, and she noticed his tanned face looked even thinner than formerly, and there was a suggestion of strain about his eyes and mouth. He looked down at her with shadowed eyes and said awkwardly:

'I do not know what a man can say to a girl who risked her life for him. Words are so inadequate.'

She thought that what was troubling him was shame that he owed her so great a debt when he had ceased to care for her. She said quickly:

'You're making too much out of a sheer accident. I made a sudden unexpected movement and spoiled his aim. As Selma said, it was just my bad luck to be in the way.'

'It was no accident,' he insisted gravely. 'You deliberately pushed in front of me, and that man was a dead shot. I know what you did and why. Is there not something in your Holy Book about no greater love than to give one's life . . . for a friend?'

'Oh, please!' Venice put her hand in front of her eyes to shut out his intent grey gaze that was threatening to shatter her self-control, which was none too strong in her weakened condition. She would hate

Selma to find her in tears when she returned.

'Don't say any more,' she besought him, then with an attempt to break the emotional tension building up between them, 'If he *had* got you, think what a loss that would have been to your country. I'm expendable.'

'No!' A vehement negative.

'Yes—but oh Kem, do be careful, there may be others who want to destroy you.'

'I am certain he was only an isolated malcontent,' Kem assured her. 'I run no greater risk than any other public man these days from madmen with a grievance, but they say lightning never strikes in the same place twice.' He smiled and was instantly grave again. 'But that you should be involved I find unbearable. If you had died ...' He spread his hands dramatically. 'What do you think I felt like when I saw you fall?'

'Well, naturally you were upset.' She laughed shakily. 'Anybody would be. Please don't make a tragedy out of it, Kem. I'm very much alive and well on the way to recovery.'

'But looking like the ghost of your former self.'

'Don't rub it in. I keep being told what a fright I look.'

'Fright? To me you look most lovely.'

Again she tried to laugh.

'Thank you, but I can hardly believe that.' She sobered and sighed. 'Nothing is changed.'

'That I question.' His eyes blazed with a sudden fierce hunger. 'Venice ...'

At that moment Selma returned.

'Here they are, darling.' She dropped a couple of paperbacks into Venice's lap, and set a basket of fruit on the table beside her. Sensing tension, she threw Kem an anxious glance.

'Anything wrong?' she asked.

'Why should there be?' His face was shuttered and set in its usual austere lines, his eyes had become dull. He moved back towards the door. 'But perhaps we should leave now. I am sure Venice tires easily.'

'Yes, perhaps we should,' Selma agreed. 'I'll come again before you go, darling, if you must go?' She looked at her friend interrogatively.

'Yes, I'm afraid I must,' Venice told her almost desperately.

'Oh well, I'll see you before you leave.' Selma stooped to kiss her, exuding a whiff of expensive perfume. 'Take care of yourself. Coming, Kem?'

He hesitated, then as Selma moved away, walked very deliberately towards Venice. Lifting her thin hand, he kissed her fingertips. It was a gesture of homage, almost of reverence, expressing much more than his words had done. Venice remembered the last time he had kissed her hand, on the day when he had told her he was going to marry Selma and had not expected to see her again. Her face contracted and it was with difficulty that she restrained her tears, as her eyes rested on the smooth brown head bent over her fingers. This time she knew it was a final farewell.

'Very pretty,' Selma said sarcastically, displeased by his action. 'Kem's going back to Ankara,' she told Venice. 'He stayed with me while you were on the danger list to comfort me, but now he must leave, so if you insist upon going home you won't see him again.'

Venice guessed some of her old mistrust was rising, and she managed to say brightly:

'Kem and I always seem to be saying goodbye, but this will really be the last time. Best of luck, Kem. I'll be seeing you, Selma?' She smiled reassuringly at her friend. She had no wish to repay her kindness and the still greater kindness of her father by trespassing.

'That you will,' Selma declared vehemently. 'Bye-bye for now, darling, and hurry up and get well.'

When they had gone, Venice stared at the door through which they had passed. Parting was no less poignant by repetition. She recalled in every detail Kem's spare energetic form, clad in the light jacket and narrow tie which he usually wore, giving a touch of elegance to distinguish him from the casually dressed tourists; the proudly held brown head and the grey eyes that had for a moment flared into sudden fire before Selma had come back. What had he been going to say when he was interrupted? It was the first time he had shown any feeling for her since he had parted from her on the terrace, except unwilling remorse because she had been wounded. Whatever it was, he had obviously decided it was better unsaid, for he had retreated into his former aloofness as soon as Selma had appeared.

Selma was defiantly flaunting her possession of him, and was apparently reconciled to the life he planned for her. Venice had the consolation of knowing that she had done them both an unestimable service at the expense of a ball through her shoulder, but only Kem was aware of their debt to her. That was all to the good, for if Selma knew it was not an accident her quick jealousy would have been aroused. She would grudge the admiration which she would be sure Kem would award to her for her courage and never quite forgive Venice for saving him. Venice gave a deep sigh; she would carry the scar of her wound for the rest of her life, but the scar upon her heart was not visible, though it was the residue of a much deeper hurt.

The Professor and his daughter visited her again next day, and continued to press her to accept their hospitality. She steadfastly refused, for when she was well enough to be discharged, she would be well enough to go home, she insisted, and it was not fair to her aunt to keep her hanging about Istanbul when she wanted to go back. They gave up in the end, and Lucas Hadleigh gave his assistance to Miss Franklin to book reservations for them on a flight to London.

Her aunt consented to unpack one of her cases and brought her some of her clothes, since those she had worn to the airport formerly were for the most part irreparable. Venice had dressed for the first time and was sitting on the balcony when she had a most unexpected visitor. Ahmet was brought out to her.

'Good lord!' she exclaimed, staring at him, in astonishment, 'I was told you were in Germany.'

He was looking very handsome and debonair in a brightly coloured shirt and cream trousers, and he presented her with a large box of Turkish Delight.

'Sweets to the sweet,' he said gallantly, and explained that Germany was not so far off that he could not return for a few days if he so desired.

'When one's only brother has been potted at by a lunatic, naturally one wishes to find out for oneself if he really is all right,' he declared airily. 'Kem is always close as a clam about himself and Mother's account was a little garbled. I find, however, that you were the single casualty—quite a distinction,' he smiled mockingly. 'What was our airport security doing?'

'Their best, I'm sure,' Venice returned. 'It can't be easy with all those crowds milling about, but Kem is in Ankara, and he wasn't touched.'

'So I have discovered, and poor Selma is practically in purdah at the Villa Yasmin with no one to escort her about except her worthy father. But I will soon alter all that.'

His bold dark eyes were studying her audaciously in a way she did not like, and she was glad that there were

166

other patients on the balcony, though at a little distance from them.

'I don't see what you can do for her,' she said uneasily, adding pointedly: 'you're not her fiancé.'

'But I cannot let the poor little thing pine away,' he announced cheerfully. 'After all, she is my cousin as well as Kem's. If he does not like it he should stay at home and look after his property. I am only consoling her for his neglect by giving her a little amusement. I arrived last night and we sampled some of those places along the Bosphorus. The wilting blossom began to bloom again. But enough of Selma—I have come to see you. To continue the floral simile, you look like a lily that has been soaked by the rain.'

'Thank you very much, that's a pretty way of saying that I look washed out!'

'It was intended as a compliment. You are all white and gold and a little pathetic. That short hair is like a halo. It shows the charming lines of your head and neck, and it is beginning to curl delectably.'

Venice flushed under his analytical stare.

'What's all this in aid of, Ahmet? I don't imagine you've come here merely to pay me compliments.'

'Must I have an ulterior motive? Naturally I wanted to see how you were for myself. Selma said you looked like a walking corpse, but she always exaggerates.' He pulled up a chair and sat down beside her. Once his masculine sexuality had excited her a little, but she was immune now, and his admiration, whether real or assumed, stimulated her ego; it was pleasant to suppose she had not become wholly unattractive.

'We started quite a promising friendship,' Ahmet went on softly. 'Until Kem spoilt it all by wafting you off to Russia, and then in the end he chose Selma.'

'Who wouldn't?' Venice returned. 'She's so lovely.'

'I think I told you once she's too obvious. Now I

have a penchant for fragile blondes, and I thought Kem had too.'

She turned her head away, wishing he would not talk about Kem.

'I never was in the running,' she said shortly.

'Why not? You are healthy and beautiful, yes? What more can a man want?'

'I'm also English and dowerless,' she reminded him.

'Oh, we are all international nowadays, and Kem does not need to be mercenary.'

'What about that cruise ship he wants capital to build?'

'The Professor Bey is going to supply that. You do not suppose he would make his daughter part of the bargain?'

Venice had thought so and looked her surprise.

Ahmet laughed. 'Those two do not mix business with romance. But since Kem is lost to you, would you allow me to console you?' The beautiful dark eyes had their most melting expression.

'I'm afraid that's impossible. I'm going back to England almost at once.'

'You must not do that. I understand you can go to the Villa Yasmin, they have asked you, yes? Please to come, Venice. I will prolong my stay to ensure that you are not bored.'

His voice sank to a pleading note, and Venice laughed.

'I'm afraid you're a flirt, Ahmet, but it's not possible. There are many reasons why I must return to England as soon as possible.'

He considered her with a gleam in his dark eyes. Venice suspected uncomfortably that he divined more of the situation than she wanted him to know; his observations had indicated that. Also she felt disquieted on Selma's account. With Kem away and his handsome brother on the doorstep she might be very indiscreet—had already been so, if she was allowing Ahmet to take her out. But she had no intention of remaining to provide a counter-attraction. That was asking too much of her; besides, there was her aunt to consider.

'Shouldn't you go back to Germany?' she asked bluntly.

'I will go when it suits me,' Ahmet returned imperturbably. 'So I cannot persuade you to delay your departure?'

'I'm afraid not.'

'Even to chaperone Selma?' he asked slyly. 'I believe that was your original function?'

'Selma has got her father and Zubeyde to look after her,' Venice pointed out. 'And she's old enough to look after herself.'

It was no use worrying about Selma, she was no longer any responsibility of hers. After tomorrow her association with the Hadleighs and Osmans would be sundered.

'Selma will never be able to take care of herself,' Ahmet predicted. 'She needs a man's control, and I doubt if my dear brother is the right man.'

'Isn't that their business?' Venice asked sweetly. Ahmet looked mischievous, and she frowned at him. 'Ahmet, you won't try to put a spoke in their wheel?'

'A what? I am not a wheelwright.'

She did not know if he were really unfamiliar with the idiom or was being deliberately obtuse.

'I mean ... interfere in any way,' she amended anxiously.

'Darling, do you believe I am so fickle?' he asked with pretended hurt. He leaned nearer, putting his hand on the arm of her chair.

'Yes,' she said, drawing away from him. 'It's a case

of how happy could I be with either.'

'Venice, you are cruel, yes?' He was enjoying himself. 'Do you not think you should stay to protect Kem's betrothed?'

She sighed at his persistence and was about to reply with a vigorous denial, when she saw that he had removed his hand and was staring at a point over her shoulders.

'Allah preserve me! Who is the gargoyle?'

Venice twisted round and saw that her aunt was standing in the doorway into her room.

'That is my Aunt Joan who has come out here to take me home.'

'That such an aunt could produce such a niece!'

'She didn't, my parents produced me. Hi, Auntie, come and meet Mrs Osman's son, Ahmet.'

Ahmet got to his feet and looked wildly round as if seeking an avenue of escape, but Miss Franklin had come forward to stand in front of them. She surveyed Ahmet grimly.

'I've met your mother,' she told him. 'She spoke about you, but she said you were away studying or something. What are you doing here with Vera?'

Ahmet recovered himself. 'Please sit down, lady.' He indicated the chair he had vacated. Aunt Joan viewed its proximity to Venice's suspiciously and did not avail herself of his invitation. He went on blithely: 'I looked in to say goodbye. I understand you insist upon taking her away from us.'

'I certainly would advise her to keep away from you. Your sort aren't any good to an honest girl,' Joan Franklin said rudely. 'But if Vera wanted to stay I wouldn't stop her. She'll be thankful to get out of Turkey after being half murdered, won't you, Vera, and why it's called that I can't imagine. I haven't seen any of those birds about.'

'It is Turkiye,' Ahmet murmured, eyeing her fearfully. 'Nothing to do with birds, and people are murdered in other countries, including your own.'

'Now don't you say anything against England, young man,' Miss Franklin scolded. 'I'd sooner live there than in these heathenish parts. At least I know what people are saying.'

'That must be a great advantage,' Ahmet agreed, deciding to take the gaunt angular woman as a joke. 'But Ven ... or did you say Vera ... will always have tender recollections of this land, yes?'

The glance he gave her was cunning, and Venice, knowing he suspected her love for Kem, hoped he would make no embarrassing remarks in front of her aunt. She had managed to successfully conceal from her that she took any interest in his brother.

'Maybe,' Aunt Joan said indifferently. 'But if she'd spent her time looking for a job instead of junketing around here as she should have done, then none of this would have happened.'

'How true.' Ahmet gave Venice another knowing look. 'And perhaps she wishes she had not, but we are directed by our fate.' Aunt Joan snorted. 'I assure you she could not help herself.'

'Rubbish!' the elder woman said loudly.

'Far be it from me to contradict you,' Ahmet said blandly. Then, tiring of the exchange: 'Ah well, if I cannot persuade you to stay, Vera-Venice, I must say goodbye.'

He bent over Venice, holding out his hand, and she took it, for after all he was Kem's half-brother. He held it longer than was necessary, gave her a soulful look, bowed to Miss Franklin and sauntered away down the terrace.

'Well, he's a Don Juan if ever there was one,' Aunt Joan observed discerningly.

'You may well be right,' Venice agreed, hoping Ahmet would respect his brother's engagement. 'I shall be glad to be home,' she observed, and meant it.

'You won't be half as glad as I'll be,' her aunt told her. 'And to think people go abroad for pleasure!'

Venice was a little anxious about her bill for hospital services, for she was not sure if her accident insurance would cover it, and she was determined not to accept any help from the Hadleighs. They had already been far too generous to her, but when she went to see the secretary, the pleasant grey-haired woman said she did not owe anything.

'But how can that be?' Venice asked doubtfully, wondering if the Hadleighs had forestalled her. 'I've been here for quite a while, had masses of treatment, a private room, everything.'

The woman looked at her solicitiously, noting how thin and wan she appeared.

'Yet you seem in a great hurry to leave. You should have stayed longer. You don't look fit to travel.'

'Oh, I'm fine,' Venice insisted. 'I'll only have to sit in a plane when all's said and done, but my bill——?'

'There isn't one. You've been the guest of the Turkish Government,' the secretary told her firmly. 'It is the least we could do for you in the circumstances.'

Kemal, Venice thought immediately. He alone knew what she had done. He was connected with the government, and this was his thank-you. She flushed and paled; she did not want to accept charity, but she knew neither she nor her aunt had the means to justify refusing it. But she might be wrong; she had been shot by a Turk on Turkish soil and her expenses might be considered reparation. In that case shouldn't she have to sign forms and what not? She realised the woman was eyeing her curiously and wondered what she had been told.

'Quite satisfied?' the woman asked.

'Please thank the Turkish Government very much on my behalf,' Venice requested.

A car would be available to take her and Miss Franklin to the airport in the morning, she was informed.

'May I wish you bon voyage?' the woman concluded.

'Thank you, you're very kind,' Venice said mechanically.

So that was that.

The airport recalled to Venice vividly that day when she was wounded. The Turkish chauffeur helped them with their baggage, and as she stood at the check-in counter, she caught herself glancing apprehensively at the crowd behind her. Then before they passed through into the departure lounge, there was a commotion among it and Selma pushed her way through to her.

'Ven, I was afraid I'd miss you. We went to the hospital and they told us you had just gone. Darling, I had to say goodbye.'

We? Venice's glance went to the crowd behind Selma, searching for a spruce agile figure. With a sense of shock she saw Ahmet.

'Ahmet brought you?'

'Yes.' Selma giggled. 'He's in no hurry to return to Germany and he's been so kind and obliging.'

She was looking radiant in sharp contrast to Venice's pallor. Ahmet came forward and took her hand.

'This is only au revoir, Venice,' he told her, his bold eyes raking her slim figure. 'You will come again, yes? I shall be desolate when Selma is married.'

Miss Franklin intervened. 'Not if I know it, young man,' she declared. 'Look what your crazy country has done to her!' She surveyed her niece grimly and certainly Venice was no advertisement for her holiday. 'She'll stop at home in future.'

Selma laughed. 'Miss Franklin is quite a dragon, Ahmet, and she thinks there's no place like home.' She threw her arms round her friend. 'Take care of yourself, darling, and come again soon.'

'Be happy,' Venice whispered.

They had to go. The last Venice saw of Selma was her colourful figure waving to her as she passed through the barrier. She was clutching Ahmet's arm with her disengaged hand.

'Is that her fiancé?' asked Joan Franklin, who had been unable to disentangle the Osman relationships.

'No, his brother.'

'Loose foreign ways,' Joan Franklin declared censoriously. She had noticed Selma's familiar manner towards Ahmet. 'I've heard Turks can have several wives, but do they go in for polyandry as well?'

'Of course not, and they only have one wife since the revolution,' Venice assured her. 'Selma's very friendly with all her fiancé's family. Ahmet is like a brother.'

'Some brother!' Her aunt commented dourly.

Venice changed the subject, but she wondered. Did Kemal know that his brother had not returned to Germany and would he approve of him acting as Selma's escort? Then she dismissed the matter from her mind. The affairs of the Osman family were no concern of hers and she did not expect to meet any of them again.

CHAPTER TEN

LONDON greeted the Franklins with a spate of dull rainy weather and seemed dark and dreary after the brilliant sunshine of the Middle East. New tenants were installed in the Hadleighs' flat. Aunt Joan's was as ugly and dingy as it had always been, except for one thing. She produced the collection of rather garish souvenirs that she had purchased in Istanbul but had never shown to Venice, and distributed them about her drably furnished sitting room, where they looked out of place.

'I want my friends to know where I've been,' she explained. 'They wouldn't believe me without evidence. Wasn't I clever getting them through the Customs undetected?'

The ornaments must have been concealed amidst Miss Franklin's assortment of carrier bags and they had not been challenged at the airport when they had walked serenely through the nothing-to-declare exit. Venice forbore to tell her that their value was not great enough to necessitate paying duty.

So salvers and ash trays edged with gilt, carrying pictures of mosques and palaces, were strewn about the room, a red flag bearing the star and crescent was displayed over the fireplace, and worry beads hung beside the mantelshelf, to the wonder and admiration of Aunt Joan's scarecrow cronies.

To Venice the one bright spot in her life was her improved relationship with her aunt. Joan Franklin remained dour and touchy, but she did try to be kind.

There was a letter waiting for Venice telling her the

post she had applied for in the north had been filled, and her aunt told her:

'You mustn't rush off into a job until you're really fit, which you are not yet. I don't mind having you around the place.'

A big concession, which she followed up with unexpected attentions, bringing Venice her breakfast in bed when she had been looking what she termed 'peaky' and her arm had been painful, for though healed it still hurt at times. Once she unbent to make what her niece supposed was an apology for her harsh bringing up.

'Never had any use for kids,' she said, 'messy little monsters. I don't know how to talk to them, and you ... you were so like your mother. I hated her because she took Derek away from me and taught him her own feckless ways. Well, she's dead now, poor soul, and one mellows as one grows older. You've turned out very well, Vera, a lot better than I expected. I'm quite proud of you.'

Venice was gratified, and not being vindictive she then and there forgave her aunt for all the deprivations of her childhood.

'You were so brave coming out to Istanbul,' she told her. 'I'll never forget that. I was so thankful to have you.'

'Now that was an experience,' Aunt Joan declared with relish. 'We could do with a bit of that sunshine these days. That Mrs Osman, she had a rare old place. I wouldn't mind living in one like it, away from all this smog.'

'Not you, Auntie, you'd never leave England,' Venice told her.

'Don't suppose I'll get the chance,' Miss Franklin said, and she looked regretful.

Venice did not see Bill for some time. He was to

start the autumn term teaching at a school in the Mid-
lands and was staying there arranging lodgings and so
forth. Eventually he made a date to meet her at their
usual coffee bar. She was sitting at a table when he
came in looking bronzed and fit, and he walked right
past her before he recognised her. When he did he
came up to her with a face of consternation.

'Ven! My dear girl, what on earth have you been
doing to yourself?'

She recalled that she had never written to tell him
about her illness, and realised that her appearance
must have given him a shock when he expected her to
be bonny and tanned by the southern sun. She explained that she had had a fever but did not mention
the incident that had caused it.

'I suppose you drank some unboiled water or something stupid,' he said perfunctorily, and Venice did not
deny it. He brought her coffee and ordered the
omelette that she requested, and then embarked upon
his own doings, which were what really interested him.
He had obtained a good post and was very pleased with
himself. While he talked, Venice studied him thoughtfully, comparing him with Kem. Feature by feature he
was handsomer than the other man, being an average
good-looking young Englishman, but he lacked Kem's
intense vitality, the force and drive that made him an
outstanding personality. Bill would be overlooked in
a crowd, Kemal would attract attention wherever he
went.

The omelettes were produced and eaten, then Bill
leaned back in his hard seat and regarded her sheep-
ishly.

'I ... er ... have some news for you,' he began, and
stopped. 'You'll never guess, and I hope you won't
mind,' he went on, and again paused.

'I probably can,' Venice told him. 'You met some

brawny Amazon in the mountains and you're thinking of becoming engaged.'

'She wasn't brawny,' he objected indignantly. 'She's beautiful, all long legs and long hair.' He glanced involuntarily at Venice's shorn locks, which though disguised by a hat, were obviously no longer shoulder-length as they used to be. 'But I ... you ... how did you know?'

'It was predictable,' she said calmly.

'You ... er ... don't mind?'

She smiled sadly. 'Not if you're happy, Bill.'

'It's very nice of you to take it like this, Ven. I mean, I thought you expected ... and I *was* quite keen on you.'

'But I went away and you found someone you liked better. Don't worry, Bill, we weren't really suited, we didn't care for the same things.'

'We didn't, did we?' he agreed with obvious relief. 'You always wanted to go abroad for holidays, which I'd hate, and you weren't a climber. Susie, that's her name, is great. You should see her on a rock face! Made me sweat to keep up with her. She's a teacher too, history and English. Of course it'll be a long time before we can get married.'

Venice laid her hand over his. 'Don't leave it too long, Bill.'

'What do you mean? One has to be practical.'

'Then be practical together—you'll both be earning, not apart. Wait too long and you may lose each other.'

Something in her voice caught his attention, and he noticed the wistful sadness in her eyes. She had changed, was not the confident carefree girl she had been when she went away.

'Something's happened to you too, hasn't it?' he asked perceptively. 'You've met someone else?'

She turned her head away. 'Don't try to probe, Bill. It's finished. Let's talk about Susie.'

'Hard cheese,' he said gently. 'So it wasn't only the fever that pulled you down. But now you've come back you'll soon regain your health and spirits, and I hope you land a bumper job.'

'Thank you, work is always a panacea,' she observed.

'Well, that lets me out,' he remarked wryly. 'I'd hate to think I'd caused any girl to look as you're looking.'

'Really, that's the fever,' she insisted, not wanting to admit that she was pining. 'Do I look so dreadful?'

'I didn't mean that. You're awfully pale, but you've acquired a kind of elusive charm, an almost fairy quality . . .'

She winced violently. 'Oh no, not that!'

'Sorry.' Bill was taken aback. 'Was I being too flowery?'

Venice had recovered herself. 'No, it was a pretty compliment.' She smiled sweetly. 'It happened to touch a sore spot, that was all.' She moved uneasily, her arm was aching. 'Shall we go? These seats aren't exactly luxurious.'

They walked in the park in the muted September afterglow. The evenings were beginning to close in. Bill chatted away about his job and his girl, and Venice listened abstractedly. In Ankara the sun would still be hot, and Selma must have fixed her wedding day. As soon as she was told the date she must send them a present . . . Selma and Kem, her heart contracted. Would she ever get over it?

Bill saw her to her bus, after promising to introduce her to Susie, probably at half term when they planned to come to London. He assured her that they must always be friends, but he did not date her again. She was a chapter of his life he had written off and he was relieved to be quit of her without reproaches.

Another door had closed, Venice thought as she tried to protect her injured shoulder from being jostled in the crowded bus. It was about time one opened; probably it would take the form of a job, but she did not view the prospect with much enthusiasm. There would be more strangers to encounter and problems to settle, but there would be children. She would like to work with little ones. In that it seemed she was going to be successful, for after the autumn term had started she was interviewed for a position in a small private school and told she might start after Christmas. It was situated near London and she would be able to spend her weekends with her aunt, who was beginning to depend increasingly upon her.

She had written to Selma several times but had had no replies. Selma was a bad correspondent, but Venice was hurt not to have received as much as a postcard from her. She wondered if she had managed to persuade Kem to modernise the house which she had so disliked and drop the teaching notion, and surely, occupied as she might be with her preparations, she would have found time to tell her when the wedding was? Venice thought of writing to the Professor to ask if she were ill, but decided it would be wiser not to. If Selma had decided to drop her it would be awkward for him. Perhaps Kem had indicated that he would prefer his wife to cease to communicate with her English friend, and Selma could be easily overruled by a man. That thought hurt still more, but it was possible he would not want to be reminded of Venice and his momentary folly.

October passed with its pageantry of turning leaves, November came in wrapping the city in dingy murk. Venice had been out upon an errand for her aunt. She returned after a brisk walk through the streets as the short daylight was fading. The exercise had brought a little colour into her pale cheeks from which the summer tan had long since faded and brightened her eyes. She had been wearing a head-scarf and she took it off as she entered the house. Her hair had grown into a crop of curls all over her head, like those of 'Bubbles' in the famous picture, she decided. Her aunt met her in the narrow hall with a severe expression.

'There's a fellow called to see you,' she told her.

Venice was hanging up her coat on the hall stand.

'If it's someone about a job I'm fixed up now,' she said.

'I don't know what he wants. Wouldn't give his name nor his business, but he looks quite respectable,' Aunt Joan conceded. 'He's waiting in the front room.'

Venice smoothed down the green pinafore dress she was wearing over a white silk blouse—Aunt Joan did not approve of trousers for women. She glanced at the small mirror set in the hall stand and ran a comb through her hair.

'Don't waste time titivating,' her aunt snapped. 'You're quite tidy. Don't need any of that muck on your face neither,' as Venice replaced the comb in her bag and pulled out a lipstick. 'He's only one of those pushing salesmen wanting to sell you some rubbish, but I thought perhaps you'd like to see him.'

'Oh yes, I did enquire about an encyclopedia,' Venice remembered, 'but I thought you said he wouldn't state his business.'

'Not to me he wouldn't, he knows I'm not gullible,' Aunt Joan declared. 'Don't you go wasting a lot on books, you haven't got it to spare.'

She stalked away down the passage, and Venice moved towards the front room door. It was an old terraced house divided into two flats, and the Franklins occupied the lower one. The tiny sitting room in front was only used when they had visitors; Aunt Joan preferred sitting in the kitchen. In it was a Raeburn stove, so it was always warm and saved fuel.

The room was lit only by the glow from the electric fire, which Venice was pleased to see her aunt had turned on—she was parsimonious about heating. The man standing in front of it was only a silhouette.

'All in the dark!' Venice exclaimed as she closed the door. She switched on the light.

Grey eyes met hers across the narrow space between them, and she fell back against its panels with a gasp.

'Kem!'

She could not imagine how he came to be there and thought wildly that her fever must have returned and she was having a hallucination, but her senses were more cognisant than her brain. Her eyes began to shine and her face became radiant, betraying all he needed to know to the man awaiting her.

In two strides he was across the room and she was enfolded in a suffocating embrace, while his mouth sought hers with almost wolfish hunger. In her too the dam built up by denial and repression broke, and she wound her arms around his neck, clinging to him with all her strength, her lips opening under the ardour of his. For a timeless space they stood interlocked, whys and wherefores forgotten.

An acid voice recalled them to realities.

'If you're going to behave like that, you might draw the curtains,' Aunt Joan snapped. 'What'll the neighbours think?'

She stalked across the room and pulled the dingy brown drapes over the window.

With her arms still about Kem's neck, Venice stared at her blankly.

'Not the man about the books?' her aunt enquired pointedly.

'Oh, no, no!' Venice disentangled herself from Kem.

'This is Mr Osman. Kem, this is my aunt, whom I live with—another Miss Franklin.'

'That's not the one I met at the hospital,' said Aunt Joan.

'That was my brother,' Kem told her. His face was set in all its old grim lines and Venice's heart sank.

'Is there ... has something happened to Selma?' she asked anxiously, for that seemed the only possible explanation for his presence. He had brought her bad news.

'It has.' His tone was as grim as his face.

'Oh, what? Is she ill? Is she ...' she could not say it. Selma could not be dead, all that radiant beauty extinguished.

'As far as I know she is in perfect health,' Kem said coldly.

Joan Franklin was regarding them with faintly sardonic amusement. She had noticed the change in Venice; the girl looked a different person since the visitor's arrival, with her cheeks glowing and the light of love undisguised in her brilliant eyes.

'Young man, I guess you've some explaining to do,' she said, not unkindly, 'and you'd like me to make myself scarce while you get on with it.' She moved to the door. 'Shout if you want help, Vera, I'll be in the kitchen.'

'Sit down, Kem,' Venice invited. 'She's right, you know.' She seated herself on the shiny horsehair sofa, but Kem remained standing, still staring at her with the same hungry expression. But before he could speak, the door opened again.

'I'll be making a pot of tea,' Miss Franklin told them. 'Your young man may like a cuppa, Vera.'

She withdrew, while Venice choked and laughed.

'Aunt Joan jumps to conclusions,' she said. She touched her forehead. 'I thought I must be dreaming, but she isn't the stuff of dreams. So you're quite real, Kem?'

'I thought I had demonstrated that,' he smiled. His face became stern again. 'Selma Hanim eloped—I think that is how you say it—with Ahmet. She went with him to Germany. There has been, as you can imagine, a scandal. Naturally I would not have her back after that, and I have insisted that Ahmet makes an honest woman of her—for the Professor's sake. Myself, I do not care what happens to that ...' He used a Turkish word which Venice was sure meant something rude. But his scorn roused her in her friend's defence.

'You shouldn't have left her,' she told him. 'You went off to Ankara leaving Ahmet at hand to console her for your neglect. She is vain and frivolous and easy prey for anyone who flatters her. You've only yourself to blame for not looking after her better.'

'But I do not want a wife with such failings,' Kemal returned. 'I want one who is loyal and loving, and who is ...' He smiled that swift elusive smile that always charmed her, lighting as it did his sombre features, '... prepared to give her life for me.'

'Do you know what you've said?' Venice whispered, for there was no mistaking his meaning.

'I am well aware of what I have said, and why else should I have come here?' he told her quietly. He sat down beside her, putting his arm about her waist and drawing her close to his side. 'Venice, I have fought this thing between us, but it has conquered me,' he began hoarsely. 'I cannot do without you. You know well enough it is madness, mistaken folly, unsuitable—we are poles apart in essentials. Do you not think I have gone over it a hundred times seeking a solution? There is none that would sound reasonable to your Western ears. I cannot compromise. You will have to capitulate completely, live in my house in Ankara that Selma de-

184

clared was not fit for human habitation. You will have to give up your nationality and accept mine, accept too my way of life. If you cannot do it, say so, and I will go away. It is a great deal to ask of any woman of different birth and breeding.'

But he still held her clamped to his side.

'Haven't you left something out?' Venice asked mischievously.

'Is not that enough?'

'Your wife was to teach English, wasn't she? I'm fully trained to teach and I hold better qualifications than Selma has.'

'And you desire to pursue your career?'

'Not particularly. Oh, Kem, none of this matters if you love me, and I . . . haven't I proved that I love you?'

Then at last he began to relax, making one last protest.

'My darling, we shall be taking a terrible chance.'

'Nothing is worse than being parted from you,' she assured him with feverish intensity. 'The time since you told me you were going to marry Selma has been sheer hell.'

'And for me too. I will never forget how you looked in that hospital, so white and frail, and it was all because of me. I wanted to take you away, cherish you, and I had tied myself to that . . .' He broke off and with his free hand began to stroke her soft hair. 'I see it is growing again, and what lovely curls!' He twisted one round his finger. 'I did not love Selma, you know that, it was a convenient arrangement.'

'Yes, I know that. But I have no endowment, Kem, only myself to offer.'

'That is riches beyond price,' he declared, falling into oriental imagery, 'but have you no stipulations to make? No conditions to demand?'

'Yes, one.'

'Ah!' He drew away from her, looking dubious. 'Something to which I can agree, I hope?'

'It's my aunt,' Venice explained. 'Lately she has changed towards me, and she is getting old. I think she leans upon me. I don't like leaving her alone.'

'The dragon who has offered us tea? But of course we must provide for her. A good Turkish family always considers its dependants. Would she like to live by the Bosphorus? There is room in Zubeyde's house and I am told they took to each other.'

Kemal had stood up and was prowling about the room.

'This is ugly,' he pronounced. 'And these objects ...' 'He picked up one of Aunt Joan's souvenirs. 'If you had wanted mementoes of Turkiye I could have given you something better than this.'

'That's my aunt's choice,' Venice told him. 'She thinks all those objects, as you call them, are marvellous.'

'Then she has already a liking for my country. Perhapse she will not be difficult to persuade. But we have talked enough about her. Come here, my beloved.'

Venice stood up and went into his arms, and rapture rose and overwhelmed her. Against his cheek she murmured shyly:

'It's a strange thing, Kem but I've always felt an affinity between us, as if we'd known each other in past ages.'

She half expected him to laugh, but he said seriously:

'We probably did. I too seemed to recognise you. In that case it was useless to fight against fate.'

He suddenly pushed her away from him, his brow darkening:

'I am forgetting. There was another fellow, Bill I

think you called him. You said you were going to marry him.'

'You can keep on forgetting him,' Venice told him happily. 'I had no intention of marrying him, that was a bit of camouflage to save my face when you rejected me. He's got himself another woman, who'll suit him a lot better than I would have done.'

'But he has kissed you ... made love to you?'

'Not really, we neither of us were keen on necking. His kisses never meant anything to me.' She gave him a sweet and tender smile. 'I was asleep until you woke me and showed me what love is.'

'Excellent!' he exclaimed, and drew her close again. 'And I will continue with your tuition, my fairy's child.'

A loud rapping on the door brought them back to place and time. Reluctantly they drew apart.

The door opened discreetly, a mere chink.

'Aren't you coming?' Aunt Joan demanded. 'Tea's getting cold.'

'Coming,' Venice told her. She gave Kem a mischievous smile. 'We must join her.' She linked her arm through his. 'Now you're going to have something that'll test your manners. I don't believe you'll appreciate a cup of real English chal'

Harlequin Announces the COLLECTION EDITIONS OF 1978

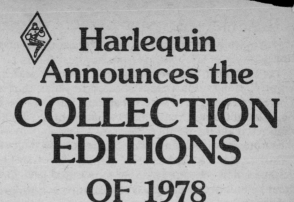

Harlequin's Collection 1?

ANDREA BLAKE
Night of the Hurrica

Harlequin's Collection 106   1.25

ANNE WEALE
If This Is Love

stories of special beauty and significance

25 Beautiful stories of particular merit

In 1976 we introduced the first 100 Harlequin Collections — a selection of titles chosen from our best sellers of the past 20 years. This series, a trip down memory lane, proved how great romantic fiction can be timeless and appealing from generation to generation. Perhaps because the theme of love and romance is eternal, and, when placed in the hands of talented, creative, authors whose true gift lies in their ability to write from the heart, the stories reach a special level of brilliance that the passage of time cannot dim. Like a treasured heirloom, an antique of superb craftsmanship, a beautiful gift from someone loved, — these stories too, have a special significance that transcends the ordinary.

Here's your 1978 Harlequin Collection Editions . . .

Send for your copy today!

The Harlequin Romance Catalog FREE!

Here's your chance to catch up on all the wonderful Harlequin Romance novels you may have missed because the books are no longer available at your favorite booksellers.

Complete the coupon and mail it to us. By return mail, we'll send you a copy of the latest Harlequin catalog. Then you'll be able to order the books you want directly from us.

Clip and mail coupon today.